Penguin Book 2231

KU-365-836

Consider Her Ways and Others

John Wyndham was born in 1903. Until 1911 he lived in Edgbaston, Birmingham, and then in many parts of England. After a wide experience of the English preparatory school he was at Bedales from 1918 to 1921. Careers he has tried include farming, law, commercial art, and advertising, and he first started writing short stories, intended for sale, in 1925. From 1930 to 1939 he wrote stories of various kinds under different names, almost exclusively for American publications. He has also written detective novels. During the war he was in the Civil Service and afterwards in the Army. In 1946 he went back to writing stories for publication in the U.S.A. and decided to try a modified form of what is unhappily known as 'science fiction'. He wrote *The Day of the Triffids*, translated into nine languages and later filmed, and followed it with *The Kraken Wakes*, which has also been translated into several languages and adapted for broadcasting, *The Chrysalids*, *The Seeds of Time*, *The Midwich Cuckoos*, (filmed as *The Village of the Damned*), *The Outward Urge*, and *Trouble with Lichen*. All have been published as Penguins.

John Wyndham

CONSIDER HER WAYS
and Others

Penguin Books
in association with Michael Joseph

Penguin Books Ltd, Harmondsworth,
Middlesex, England
Penguin Books Pty Ltd, Ringwood, Victoria,
Australia

First published by Michael Joseph 1961
Published in Penguin Books 1965

Copyright © John Wyndham 1956, 1961

Made and printed in Great Britain by Cox &
Wyman Ltd., London, Fakenham and Reading.
Set in Monotype Imprint

Contents

Consider Her Ways

There was nothing but myself.

I hung in a timeless, spaceless, forceless void that was neither light, nor dark. I had entity, but no form; awareness, but no senses; mind, but no memory. I wondered, is this – this nothingness – my soul? And it seemed that I had wondered that always, and should go on wondering it for ever. . . .

But, somehow, timelessness ceased. I became aware that there *was* a force: that I was being moved, and that spacelessness had, therefore, ceased, too. There was nothing to show that I moved; I knew simply that I was being drawn. I felt happy because I knew there was something or someone to whom I wanted to be drawn. I had no other wish than to turn like a compass-needle, and then fall through the void. . . .

But I was disappointed. No smooth, swift fall followed. Instead, other forces fastened on me. I was pulled this way, and then that. I did not know how I knew it; there was no outside reference, no fixed point, no direction, even; yet I could feel that I was tugged hither and thither, as though against the resistance of some inner gyroscope. It was as if one force were in command of me for a time, only to weaken and lose me to a new force. Then I would seem to slide towards an unknown point, until I was arrested, and diverted upon another course. I wafted this way and that, with the sense of awareness continually growing firmer; and I wondered whether rival forces were fighting for me, good and evil, perhaps, or life and death. . . .

The sense of pulling back and forth became more definite until I was almost jerked from one course to another. Then abruptly, the feeling of struggle finished. I had a sense of travelling faster and faster still, plunging like a wandering meteorite that had been trapped at last. . . .

'All right,' said a voice, 'Resuscitation was a little retarded, for some reason. Better make a note of that on her card. What's the number? Oh, only her fourth time. Yes, certainly make a note. It's all right. Here she comes!'

It was a woman's voice speaking, with a slightly unfamiliar accent. The surface I was lying on shook under me. I opened my eyes, saw the ceiling moving along above me, and let them close. Presently, another voice, again with an unfamiliar intonation, spoke to me:

'Drink this,' she said.

A hand lifted my head, and a cup was pressed against my lips. After I had drunk the stuff I lay back with my eyes closed again. I dozed for a little while, and came out of it feeling stronger. For some minutes I lay looking up at the ceiling and wondering vaguely where I was. I could not recall any ceiling that was painted just this pinkish shade of cream. Then, suddenly, while I was still gazing up at the ceiling, I was shocked, just as if something had hit my mind a sharp blow. I was frighteningly aware that it was not just the pinkish ceiling that was unfamiliar – *everything* was unfamiliar. Where there should have been memories there was just a great gap. I had no idea who I was, or where I was; I could recall nothing of how or why I came to be here. . . . In a rush of panic I tried to sit up, but a hand pressed me back, and presently held the cup to my lips again.

'You're quite all right. Just relax,' the same voice told me, reassuringly.

I wanted to ask questions, but somehow I felt immensely weary, and everything was too much trouble. The first rush of panic subsided, leaving me lethargic. I wondered what had happened to me – had I been in an accident, perhaps? Was this the kind of thing that happened when one was badly shocked? I did not know, and now for the moment I did not care: I was being looked after. I felt so drowsy that the questions could wait.

I suppose I dozed, and it may have been for a few minutes, or for an hour. I know only that when I opened my eyes again I felt calmer – more puzzled than alarmed – and I lay for a time without moving. I had recovered enough grasp now to console myself with the thought that if there had been an accident, at least there was no pain.

Presently I gained a little more energy, and, with it, curiosity to know where I was. I rolled my head on the pillow to see more of the surroundings.

A few feet away I saw a contrivance on wheels, something between a bed and a trolley. On it, asleep with her mouth open, was the most enormous woman I had ever seen. I stared, wondering whether it was some kind of cage over her to take the weight of the covers that gave her the mountainous look, but the movement of her breathing soon showed me that it was not. Then I looked beyond her and saw two more trolleys, both supporting equally enormous women.

I studied the nearest one more closely, and discovered to my surprise that she was quite young – not more than twenty-two, or twenty-three, I guessed. Her face was a little plump, perhaps, but by no means over-fat; indeed, with her fresh, healthy young colouring and her short-cropped gold curls, she was quite pretty. I fell to wondering what curious disorder of the glands could cause such a degree of anomaly at her age.

Ten minutes or so passed, and there was a sound of brisk, businesslike footsteps approaching. A voice inquired:

'How are you feeling now?'

I rolled my head to the other side, and found myself looking into a face almost level with my own. For a moment I thought its owner must be a child, then I saw that the features under the white cap were certainly not less than thirty years old. Without waiting for a reply she reached under the bedclothes and took my pulse. Its rate appeared to satisfy her, for she nodded confidently.

'You'll be all right now, Mother,' she told me.

I stared at her, blankly.

'The car's only just outside the door there. Do you think you can walk it?' she went on.

Bemusedly, I asked:

'What car?'

'Why, to take you home, of course,' she said, with professional patience. 'Come along now.' And she pulled away the bedclothes.

I started to move, and looked down. What I saw there held me fixed. I lifted my arm. It was like nothing so much as a plump, white bolster with a ridiculous little hand attached at the end. I stared at it in horror. Then I heard a far-off scream as I fainted. . . .

When I opened my eyes again there was a woman – a normal-sized woman – in a white overall with a stethoscope round her neck, frowning at me in perplexity. The white-capped woman I had taken for a child stood beside her, reaching only a little above her elbow.

'— I don't know, Doctor,' she was saying. 'She just suddenly screamed, and fainted.'

'What is it? What's happened to me? I know I'm not like this – I'm not, I'm not,' I said, and I could hear my own voice wailing the words.

The doctor went on looking puzzled.

'What does she mean?' she asked.

'I've no idea, Doctor,' said the small one. 'It was quite sudden, as if she'd had some kind of shock – but I don't know why.'

'Well, she's been passed and signed off, and, anyway, she can't stay here. We need the room,' said the doctor. 'I'd better give her a sedative.'

'But what's happened? Who am I? There's something terribly wrong. I know I'm not like this. P-please t-tell me –' I implored her, and then somehow lost myself in a stammer and a muddle.

The doctor's manner became soothing. She laid a hand gently on my shoulder.

'That's all right, Mother. There's nothing to worry about. Just take things quietly. We'll soon have you back home.'

Another white-capped assistant, no taller than the first, hurried up with a syringe, and handed it to the doctor.

'No!' I protested. 'I want to know where I am. Who am I? Who are you? What's happened to me?' I tried to slap the syringe out of her hand, but both the small assistants flung themselves on my arm, and held on to it while she pressed in the needle.

It was a sedative, all right. It did not put me out, but it detached me. An odd feeling: I seemed to be floating a few feet outside myself and considering me with an unnatural calmness. I was able, or felt that I was able, to evaluate matters with intelligent clarity. . . .

Evidently I was suffering from amnesia. A shock of some kind had caused me to 'lose my memory', as it is often put. Obviously it was only a very small part of my memory that had gone – just the personal part, who I was, what I was, where I lived – all the mechanism for day to day getting along seemed to be intact: I'd not forgotten how to talk, or how to think, and I seemed to have quite a well-stored mind to think with.

On the other hand there was a nagging conviction that everything about me was somehow *wrong*. I *knew*, somehow, that I'd never before seen the place I was in; I *knew*, too, that there was something queer about the presence of the two small nurses; above all, I *knew*, with absolute certainty, that this massive form lying here was not mine. I could not recall what face I ought to see in a mirror, not even whether it would be dark or fair, or old or young, but there was no shadow of doubt in my mind that whatever it was like, it had never topped such a shape as I had now.

– And there were the other enormous young women, too. Obviously, it could not be a matter of glandular disorder in all of us, or there'd not be this talk of sending me 'home', wherever that might be. . . .

I was still arguing the situation with myself in, thanks no

11

doubt to the sedative, a most reasonable-seeming manner, though without making any progress at all, when the ceiling above my head began to move again, and I realized I was being wheeled along. Doors opened at the end of the room, and the trolley tilted a little beneath me as we went down a gentle ramp beyond.

At the foot of the ramp, an ambulance-like car, with pink coachwork polished until it gleamed, was waiting with the rear doors open. I observed interestedly that I was playing a part in a routine procedure. A team of eight diminutive attendants carried out the task of transferring me from the trolley to a sprung couch in the ambulance as if it were a kind of drill. Two of them lingered after the rest to tuck in my coverings and place another pillow behind my head. Then they got out, closing the doors behind them, and in a minute or two we started off.

It was at this point – and possibly the sedative helped in this, too – that I began to have an increasing sense of balance and a feeling that I was perceiving the situation. Probably there *had* been an accident, as I had suspected, but obviously my error, and the chief cause of my alarm, proceeded from my assumption that I was a stage further on than I actually was. I had assumed that after an interval I had recovered consciousness in these baffling circumstances, whereas the true state of affairs must clearly be that I had *not* recovered consciousness. I must still be in a suspended state, very likely with concussion, and this was a dream, or hallucination. Presently, I should wake up in conditions that would at least be sensible, if not necessarily familiar.

I wondered now that this consoling and stabilizing thought had not occurred to me before, and decided that it was the alarming sense of detailed reality that had thrown me into panic. It had been astonishingly stupid of me to be taken in to the extent of imagining that I really was a kind of Gulliver among rather oversize Lilliputians. It was quite characteristic of most dreams, too, that I should lack a clear knowledge of my identity, so we did not need to be surprised at that. The thing to do was to take an intelligent interest in all I observed: the whole thing must be chockful of symbolic content which it would be most interesting to work out later.

The discovery quite altered my attitude and I looked about me with a new attention. It struck me as odd right away that there was so much circumstantial detail, and all of it in focus – there was none of that sense of foreground in sharp relief against a muzzy, or even non-existent, background that one usually meets in a dream. Everything was presented with a most convincing, three-dimensional solidity. My own sensations, too, seemed perfectly valid. The injection, in particular, had been quite acutely authentic. The illusion of reality fascinated me into taking mental notes with some care.

The interior of the van, or ambulance, or whatever it was, was finished in the same shell-pink as the outside – except for the roof, which was powder-blue with a scatter of small silver stars. Against the front partition were mounted several cupboards, with plated handles. My couch, or stretcher, lay along the left side: on the other were two fixed seats, rather small, and upholstered in a semi-glazed material to match the colour of the rest. Two long windows on each side left little solid wall. Each of them was provided with curtains of a fine net, gathered back now in pink braid loops, and had a roller blind furled above it. Simply by turning my head on the pillow I was able to observe the passing scenery – though somewhat jerkily, for either the springing of the vehicle scarcely matched its appointments, or the road surface was bad: whichever the cause, I was glad my own couch was independently and quite comfortably sprung.

The external view did not offer a great deal of variety save in its hues. Our way was lined by buildings standing back behind some twenty yards of tidy lawn. Each block was three storeys high, about fifty yards long, and had a tiled roof of somewhat low pitch, suggesting a vaguely Italian influence. Structurally the blocks appeared identical, but each was differently coloured, with contrasting window-frames and doors, and carefully-considered, uniform curtains. I could see no one behind the windows, indeed there appeared to be no one about at all except here and there a woman in overalls mowing a lawn, or tending one of the inset flower-beds.

Farther back from the road, perhaps two hundred yards away, stood larger, taller, more utilitarian-looking blocks, some of them with high, factory-type chimneys. I thought they might actually be factories of some kind, but at the distance, and because I had no more than fugitive views of them between the foreground blocks, I could not be sure.

The road itself seldom ran straight for more than a hundred yards at a stretch, and its windings made one wonder whether the builders had not been more concerned to follow a contour line than a direction. There was little other traffic, and what there was consisted of lorries, large or small, mostly large. They were painted in one primary colour or other, with only a five-fold combination of letters and figures on their sides for further identification. In design they might have been any lorries anywhere.

We continued this uneventful progress at a modest pace for some twenty minutes, until we came to a stretch where the road was under repair. The car slowed, and the workers moved to one side, out of our way. As we crawled forward over the broken surface I was able to get a good look at them. They were all women or girls dressed in denim-like trousers, sleeveless singlets, and working boots. All had their hair cut quite short, and a few wore hats. They were tall and broad-shouldered, bronzed and healthy-looking. The biceps of their arms were like a man's, and the hafts of their picks and shovels rested in the hard, strong hands of manual toilers.

They watched with concern as the car edged its way on to the rough patch, but when it drew level with them they transferred their attention, and jostled and craned to look inside at me.

They smiled widely, showing strong white teeth in their browned faces. All of them raised their right hands, making some sign to me, still smiling. Their goodwill was so evident that I smiled back. They walked along, keeping pace with the crawling car, looking at me expectantly while their smiles faded into puzzlement. They were saying something but I could not hear the words. Some of them insistently repeated the sign. Their disappointed look made it clear that I was expected to respond with more than a smile. The only way that occurred to me was to raise my own right hand in imitation of their gesture. It was at least a qualified success; their faces brightened though a rather puzzled look remained. Then the car lurched on to the made-up road again, and their still somewhat troubled faces slid back as we speeded up to our former sedate pace. More dream symbols, of course – but certainly not one of the stock symbols from the book. What on earth, I wondered, could a party of friendly Amazons, equipped with navvying implements instead of bows, stand for in my subconscious? Something frustrated, I imagined. A suppressed desire to dominate? I did not seem to be getting much farther along that line when we passed the last of the variegated but nevertheless monotonous blocks, and ran into open country.

The flower-beds had shown me already that it was spring, and now I was able to look on healthy pastures, and neat arable fields already touched with green; there was a haze like green smoke along the trim hedges, and some of the trees in the tidily placed spinneys were in young leaf. The sun was shining with a bright benignity upon the most precise countryside I had ever seen; only the cattle dotted about the fields introduced a slight disorder into the careful dispositions. The farmhouses themselves were part of the pattern; hollow squares of neat buildings with an acre or so of vegetable garden on one side, an orchard on another, and a rickyard on a third. There was a suggestion of a doll's landscape about it – Grandma Moses, but tidied up and rationalized. I could see no random cottages, casually sited sheds, or unplanned outgrowths from the farm buildings. And what, I asked myself, should we conclude from this rather pathological exhibition of tidiness? That I was a more uncertain person than I had supposed, one who was subconsciously yearning for simplicity and security? Well, well. . . .

An open lorry which must have been travelling ahead of us turned off down a lane bordered by beautifully laid hedges, towards one of the farms. There were half a dozen young women in it, holding implements of some kind; Amazons, again. One of them, looking back, drew the attention of the rest to us. They raised their hands in the same sign that the others had made, and then waved cheerfully. I waved back.

Rather bewildering, I thought: Amazons for domination *and* this landscape, for passive security: the two did not seem to tie up very well.

We trundled on, at our unambitious pace of twenty miles an hour or so, for what I guessed to be three-quarters of an hour, with the prospect changing very little. The country undulated gently and appeared to continue like that to the foot of a line of low, blue hills many miles away. The tidy farmhouses went by with almost the regularity of milestones, though with something like twice the frequency. Occasionally there were working-parties in the fields; more rarely, one saw individuals busy about the farm, and others hoeing with tractors, but they were all too far off for me to make out any details. Presently, however, came a change.

Off to the left of the road, stretching back at right-angles to it for more than a mile, appeared a row of trees. At first I thought it just a wood, but then I noticed that the trunks were evenly spaced, and the trees themselves topped and pruned until they gave more the impression of a high fence.

The end of it came to within twenty feet of the road, where it turned, and we ran along beside it for almost half a mile until the car slowed, turned to the left and stopped in front of a pair of tall gates. There were a couple of toots on the horn.

The gates were ornamental, and possibly of wrought iron under their pink paint. The archway that they barred was stucco-covered, and painted the same colour.

Why, I inquired of myself, this prevalence of pink, which I regard as a namby-pamby colour, anyway? Flesh-colour? Symbolic of an ardency for the flesh which I had insufficiently gratified? I scarcely thought so. Not pink. Surely a burning red . . . I don't think I know anyone who can be really ardent in a pink way. . . .

While we waited, a feeling that there was something wrong with the gatehouse grew upon me. The structure was a single-storey building, standing against the left, inner side of the archway, and coloured to match it. The woodwork was pale blue, and there were white net curtains at the windows. The door opened, and a middle-aged woman in a white blouse-and-trouser suit came out. She was bare-headed, with a few grey locks in her short, dark hair. Seeing me, she raised her hand in the same sign the Amazons had used, though perfunctorily, and walked over to open the gates. It was only as she pushed them back to admit us that I suddenly saw how small she was – certainly not over four feet tall. And that explained what was wrong with the gatehouse: it was built entirely to her scale. . . .

I went on staring at her and her little house as we passed. Well, what about that? Mythology is rich in gnomes and 'little people', and they are fairly pervasive of dreams, too, so somebody, I am sure, must have decided that they are a standard symbol of something, but for the moment I did not recall what it was. Would it be repressed philoprogenitiveness, or was that too unsubtle? I stowed that away, too, for later contemplation and brought my attention back to the surroundings.

We were on our way, unhurriedly, along something more like a drive than a road, with surroundings that suggested a compromise between a public garden and a municipal housing-estate. There were wide lawns of an unblemished velvet green, set here and there with flower-beds, delicate groups of silver birch, and occasional, larger, single trees. Among them stood pink, three-storey blocks, dotted about, seemingly to no particular plan.

A couple of the Amazon-types in singlets and trousers of a faded rust-red were engaged in planting-out a bed close beside the drive, and we had to pause while they dragged their handcart full of tulips on to the grass to let us pass. They gave me the usual salute and amiable grin as we went by.

A moment later I had a feeling that something had gone wrong with my sight, for as we passed one block we came in sight of another. It was white instead of pink, but otherwise exactly similar to the rest – except that it was scaled down by at least one-third. . . .

I blinked at it and stared hard, but it continued to seem just the same size.

A little farther on, a grotesquely huge woman in pink draperies was walking slowly and heavily across a lawn. She was accompanied by three of the small, white-suited women looking, in contrast, like children, or very animated dolls: one was involuntarily reminded of tugs fussing round a liner.

I began to feel swamped: the proliferation and combination of symbols was getting well out of my class.

The car forked to the right, and presently we drew up before a flight of steps leading to one of the pink buildings – a normal-sized building, but still not free from oddity, for the steps were divided by a central balustrade; those to the left of it were normal, those to the right, smaller and more numerous.

Three toots on the horn announced our arrival. In about ten seconds half a dozen small women appeared in the doorway and came running down the right-hand side of the steps. A door slammed as the driver got out and went to meet them. When she came into my range of view I saw that she was one of the little ones, too, but not in white as the rest were; she wore a shining pink suit like a livery that exactly matched the car.

They had a word together before they came round to open the door behind me, then a voice said brightly:

'Welcome, Mother Orchis. Welcome home.'

The couch, or stretcher, slid back on runners, and between them they lowered it to the ground. One young woman whose blouse was badged with a pink St Andrew's cross on the left breast leaned over me. She inquired considerately:

'Do you think you can walk, Mother?'

It did not seem the moment to inquire into the form of

18

address. I was obviously the only possible target for the question.

'Walk?' I repeated. 'Of course I can walk.' And I sat up, with about eight hands assisting me.

'Of course' had been an overstatement. I realized that by the time I had been heaved to my feet. Even with all the help that was going on around me it was an exertion which brought on heavy breathing. I looked down at the monstrous form that billowed under my pink draperies, with a sickly revulsion and a feeling that whatever this particular mass of symbolism disguised, it was likely to prove a distasteful revelation later on. I tried a step. 'Walk' was scarcely the word for my progress. It felt like, and must have looked like, a slow series of forward surges. The women, at little more than my elbow height, fluttered about me like a flock of anxious hens. Once started, I was determined to go on, and I progressed with a kind of wave-motion, first across a few yards of gravel, and then, with ponderous deliberation, up the left-hand side of the steps.

There was a perceptible sense of relief and triumph all round as I reached the summit. We paused there a few moments for me to regain my breath, then we moved on into the building. A corridor led straight ahead, with three or four closed doors on each side; at the end it branched right and left. We took the left arm, and, at the end of it, I came face to face, for the first time since the hallucination had set in, with a mirror.

It took every volt of my resolution not to panic again at what I saw in it. The first few seconds of my stare were spent in fighting down a leaping hysteria.

In front of me stood an outrageous travesty: an elephantine female form, looking the more huge for its pink swathings. Mercifully, they covered everything but the head and hands, but these exposures were themselves another kind of shock, for the hands, though soft and dimpled and looking utterly out of proportion, were not uncomely, and the head and face were those of a girl.

She was pretty, too. She could not have been more than twenty-one, if that. Her curling fair hair was touched with auburn lights, and cut in a kind of bob. The complexion of her face was pink and cream, her mouth was gentle, and red without any artifice. She looked back at me, and at the little women anxiously clustering round me, from a pair of blue-green eyes beneath lightly arched brows. And this delicate face, this little Fragonard, was set upon that monstrous body: no less outrageously might a blossom of freesia sprout from a turnip.

When I moved my lips, hers moved; when I bent my arm, hers bent; and yet, once I got the better of that threatening panic, she ceased to be a reflection. She was nothing like me, so she must be a stranger whom I was observing, though in a most bewildering way. My panic and revulsion gave way to sadness, an aching pity for her. I could weep for the shame of it. I did. I watched the tears brim on her lower lids; mistily, I saw them overflow.

One of the little women beside me caught hold of my hand. 'Mother Orchis, dear, what's the matter?' she asked, full of concern.

I could not tell her: I had no clear idea myself. The image in the mirror shook her head, with tears running down her cheeks. Small hands patted me here and there; small, soothing voices encouraged me onward. The next door was opened for me and I was led into the room beyond, amid concerned fussing.

We entered a place that struck me as a cross between a boudoir and a ward. The boudoir impression was sustained by a great deal of pink – in the carpet, coverlets, cushions, lampshades, and filmy window-curtains; the ward motif, by an array of six divans, or couches, one of which was unoccupied.

It was a large enough room for three couches, separated by a chest, chair and table for each, to be arranged on either side without an effect of crowding, and the open space in the middle was still big enough to contain several expansive easy-chairs and a central table bearing an intricate flower-arrangement. A not-displeasing scent faintly pervaded the place, and from somewhere came the subdued sound of a string-quartet in a sentimental mood. Five of the bed-couches were already mountainously occupied. Two of my attendant party detached themselves and hurried ahead to turn back the pink satin cover on the sixth.

Faces from all the five other beds were turned towards me. Three of them smiling in welcome, the other two less committal.

'Hallo, Orchis,' one of them greeted me in a friendly tone. Then, with a touch of concern she added: 'What's the matter, dear? Did you have a bad time?'

I looked at her. She had a kindly, plumply pretty face, framed by light-brown hair as she lay back against a cushion. The face looked about twenty-three or twenty-four years old. The rest of her was a huge mound of pink satin. I couldn't make any reply, but I did my best to return her smile as we passed.

Our convoy hove to by the empty bed. After some preparation and positioning I was helped into it by all hands, and a cushion was arranged behind my head.

The exertion of my journey from the car had been considerable, and I was thankful to relax. While two of the little women pulled up the coverlet and arranged it over me, another produced a handkerchief and dabbed gently at my cheeks. She encouraged me:

'There you are, dear. Safely home again now. You'll be quite all right when you've rested a bit. Just try to sleep for a little.'

'What's the matter with her?' inquired a forthright voice from one of the other beds. 'Did she make a mess of it?'

The little woman with the handkerchief – she was the one who wore the St Andrew's cross and appeared to be in charge of the operation – turned her head sharply.

'There's no need for that tone, Mother Hazel. Of course Mother Orchis had four beautiful babies – didn't you, dear?' she added to me. 'She's just a bit tired after the journey, that's all.'

'H'mph,' said the girl addressed, in an unaccommodating tone, but she made no further comment.

A degree of fussing continued. Presently the small woman handed me a glass of something that looked like water, but had unsuspected strength. I spluttered a little at the first taste, but quickly felt the better for it. After a little more tidying and ordering, my retinue departed leaving me propped against my cushion, with the eyes of the five other monstrous women dwelling upon me speculatively.

An awkward silence was broken by the girl who had greeted me as I came in.

'Where did they send you for your holiday, Orchis?'

'Holiday?' I asked blankly.

She and the rest stared at me in astonishment.

'I don't know what you are talking about,' I told them.

They went on staring, stupidly, stolidly.

'It can't have been much of a holiday,' observed one, obviously puzzled. 'I'll not forget my last one. They sent me to the sea, and gave me a little car so that I could get about everywhere. Everybody was lovely to us, and there were only six Mothers there, including me. Did you go by the sea, or in the mountains?'

They were determined to be inquisitive, and one would have to make some answer sooner or later. I chose what seemed the simplest way out for the moment.

'I can't remember,' I said. 'I can't remember a thing. I seem to have lost my memory altogether.'

That was not very sympathetically received, either.

'Oh,' said the one who had been addressed as Hazel, with a degree of satisfaction. 'I thought there was something. And I suppose you can't even remember for certain whether your babies were Grade One this time, Orchis?'

'Don't be stupid, Hazel,' one of the others told her. 'Of course they were Grade One. If they'd not been, Orchis wouldn't be back here now – she'd have been re-rated as a Class Two Mother, and sent to Whitewich.' In a more kindly tone she asked me: 'When did it happen, Orchis?'

'I – I don't know,' I said. 'I can't remember anything before this morning at the hospital. It's all gone entirely.'

'Hospital!' repeated Hazel, scornfully.

'She must mean the Centre,' said the other. 'But do you mean to say you can't even remember *us*, Orchis?'

'No,' I admitted, shaking my head. 'I'm sorry, but everything before I came round in the Hosp – in the Centre, is all blank.'

'That's queer,' Hazel said, in an unsympathetic tone. 'Do they know?'

One of the others took my part.

'Of course they're bound to know. I expect they don't think that remembering or not has anything to do with having Grade One babies. And why should it, anyway? But look, Orchis –'

'Why not let her rest for a bit,' another cut in. 'I don't suppose she's feeling too good after the Centre, and the journey, and getting in here. I never do myself. Don't take any notice of them, Orchis, dear. You just go to sleep for a bit. You'll probably find it's all quite all right when you wake up.'

I accepted her suggestion gratefully. The whole thing was far too bewildering to cope with at the moment; moreover, I did feel exhausted. I thanked her for her advice, and lay back on my pillow. In so far as the closing of one's eyes can be made ostentatious, I made it so. What was more surprising was that, if one can be said to sleep within an hallucination or a dream, I slept. . . .

In the moment of waking, before opening my eyes, I had a flash of hope that I should find the illusion had spent itself. Unfortunately, it had not. A hand was shaking my shoulder gently, and the first thing that I saw was the face of the little women's leader, close to mine.

In the way of nurses, she said:

'There, Mother Orchis, dear. You'll be feeling a lot better after that nice sleep, won't you?'

Beyond her, two more of the small women were carrying a short-legged bed-tray towards me. They set it down so that

23

it bridged me, and was convenient to reach. I stared at the load on it. It was, with no exception, the most enormous and nourishing meal I had ever seen put before one person. The first sight of it revolted me – but then I became aware of a schism within, for it did not revolt the physical form that I occupied: that, in fact, had a watering mouth, and was eager to begin. An inner part of me marvelled in a kind of semi-detachment while the rest consumed two or three fish, a whole chicken, some slices of meat, a pile of vegetables, fruit hidden under mounds of stiff cream, and more than a quart of milk, without any sense of surfeit. Occasional glances showed me that the other 'Mothers' were dealing just as thoroughly with the contents of their similar trays.

I caught one or two curious looks from them, but they were too seriously occupied to take up their inquisition again at the moment. I wondered how to fend them off later, and it occurred to me that if only I had a book or a magazine I might be able to bury myself effectively, if not very politely, in it.

When the attendants returned I asked the badged one if she could let me have something to read. The effect of such a simple request was astonishing: the two who were removing my tray all but dropped it. The one beside me gaped for an amazed moment before she collected her wits. She looked at me, first with suspicion, and then with concern.

'Not feeling quite yourself yet, dear?' she suggested.

'But I am,' I protested. 'I'm quite all right now.'

The look of concern persisted, however.

'If I were you I'd try to sleep again,' she advised.

'But I don't want to. I'd just like to read quietly,' I objected.

She patted my shoulder, a little uncertainly.

'I'm afraid you've had an exhausting time, Mother. Never mind, I'm sure it'll pass quite soon.'

I felt impatient. 'What's wrong with wanting to read?' I demanded.

She smiled a smug, professional-nurse smile.

'There, there, dear. Just you try to rest a little more. Why, bless me, what on earth would a Mother want with knowing how to read?'

With that she tidied my coverlet, and bustled away, leaving me to the wide-eyed stares of my five companions. Hazel gave a kind of contemptuous snigger; otherwise there was no audible comment for several minutes.

I had reached a stage where the persistence of the hallucination was beginning to wear away my detachment. I could feel that under a little more pressure I should be losing my confidence and starting to doubt its unreality. I did not at all care for its calm continuity. Inconsequent exaggerations and jumps, foolish perspectives, indeed any of the usual dream characteristics would have been reassuring, but, instead, it continued to present obvious nonsense, with an alarming air of conviction and consequence. Effects, for instance, were unmistakably following causes. I began to have an uncomfortable feeling that were one to dig deep enough one might begin to find logical causes for the absurdities, too. The integration was far too good for mental comfort – even the fact that I had enjoyed my meal as if I were fully awake, and was consciously feeling the better for it, encouraged the disturbing quality of reality.

'Read!' Hazel said suddenly, with a scornful laugh. 'And write, too, I suppose?'

'Well, why not?' I retorted.

They all gazed at me more attentively than ever, and then exchanged meaning glances among themselves. Two of them smiled at one another. I demanded irritably: 'What on earth's wrong with that? Am I supposed not to be able to read or write, or something?'

One said kindly, soothingly:

'Orchis, dear. Don't you think it would be better if you were to ask to see the doctor? – Just for a check-up?'

'No,' I told her flatly. 'There's nothing wrong with me. I'm just trying to understand. I simply ask for a book, and you all look at me as if I were mad. Why?'

After an awkward pause the same one said humouringly, and almost in the words of the little attendant:

'Orchis, dear, do try to pull yourself together. What sort of good would reading and writing be to a Mother. How could they help her to have better babies?'

'There are other things in life besides having babies,' I said, shortly.

If they had been surprised before, they were thunderstruck now. Even Hazel seemed bereft of suitable comment. Their idiotic astonishment exasperated me and made me suddenly sick of the whole nonsensical business. Temporarily, I *did* forget to be the detached observer of a dream.

'Damn it,' I broke out. 'What *is* all this rubbish? Orchis! Mother Orchis! – for God's sake! Where am I? Is this some kind of lunatic asylum?'

I stared at them, angrily, loathing the sight of them, wondering if they were all in some spiteful complicity against me. Somehow I was quite convinced in my own mind that whoever, or whatever I was, I was not a mother. I said so, forcibly, and then, to my annoyance, burst into tears.

For lack of anything else to use, I dabbed at my eyes with my sleeve. When I could see clearly again I found that four of them were looking at me with kindly concern. Hazel, however, was not.

'I said there was something queer about her,' she told the others, triumphantly. 'She's mad, that's what it is.'

The one who had been most kindly disposed before, tried again:

'But, Orchis, *of course* you are a Mother. You're a Class One Mother – with three births registered. Twelve fine Grade One babies, dear. You *can't* have forgotten that!'

For some reason I wept again. I had a feeling that something was trying to break through the blankness in my mind; but I did not know what it was, only that it made me feel intensely miserable.

'Oh, this is cruel, cruel! Why can't I stop it? Why won't it go away and leave me?' I pleaded. 'There's a horrible cruel mockery here – but I don't understand it. What's wrong with me? I'm not obsessional – I'm not – I – oh, can't somebody help me . . . ?'

I kept my eyes tight shut for a time, willing with all my mind that the whole hallucination should fade and disappear.

But it did not. When I looked again they were still there, their silly, pretty faces gaping stupidly at me across the revolting mounds of pink satin.

'I'm going to get out of this,' I said.

It was a tremendous effort to raise myself to a sitting position. I was aware of the rest watching me, wide-eyed, while I made it. I struggled to get my feet round and over the side of the bed, but they were all tangled in the satin coverlet and I could not reach to free them. It was the true, desperate frustration of a dream. I heard my voice pleading: 'Help me! Oh, Donald, darling, please help me. . . .'

And suddenly, as if the word 'Donald' had released a spring, something seemed to click in my head. The shutter in my mind opened, not entirely, but enough to let me know who I was. I understood, suddenly, where the cruelty had lain.

I looked at the others again. They were still staring half-bewildered, half-alarmed. I gave up the attempt to move, and lay back on my pillow again.

'You can't fool me any more,' I told them. 'I know who I am now.'

'But, Mother Orchis –' one began.

'Stop that,' I snapped at her. I seemed to have swung suddenly out of self-pity into a kind of masochistic callousness. 'I am *not* a mother,' I said harshly. 'I am just a woman who, for a short time, had a husband, and who hoped – but only hoped – that she would have babies by him.'

A pause followed that; a rather odd pause, where there should have been at least a murmur. What I had said did not seem to have registered. The faces showed no understanding; they were as uncomprehending as dolls.

Presently, the most friendly one seemed to feel an obligation to break up the silence. With a little vertical crease between her brows: 'What,' she inquired tentatively, 'what is a husband?'

I looked hard from one face to another. There was no trace of guile in any of them; nothing but puzzled speculation such as one sometimes sees in a child's eyes. I felt close to hysteria for a moment; then I took a grip of myself. Very well, then, since the hallucination would not leave me alone, I would play it at its own game, and see what came of that. I began to explain with a kind of deadpan, simple-word seriousness:

'A husband is a man whom a woman takes. . . .'

Evidently, from their expressions I was not very enlightening. However, they let me go on for three or four sentences without interruption. Then, when I paused for breath, the kindly one chipped in with a point which she evidently felt needed clearing up:

'But what,' she asked, in evident perplexity, 'what is a man?'

A cool silence hung over the room after my exposition. I had an impression I had been sent to Coventry, or semi-Coventry, by them, but I did not bother to test it. I was too much occupied trying to force the door of my memory further open, and finding that beyond a certain point it would not budge.

I knew now that I was Jane. I had been Jane Summers, and had become Jane Waterleigh when I had married Donald.

I was – had been – twenty-four when we were married: just twenty-five when Donald was killed, six months later. And there it stopped. It seemed like yesterday, but I couldn't tell. . . .

Before that, everything was perfectly clear. My parents and friends, my home, my school, my training, my job, as Dr Summers, at the Wraychester Hospital. I could remember my first sight of Donald when they brought him in one evening with a broken leg – and all that followed. . . .

I could remember now the face that I ought to see in a looking-glass – and it was certainly nothing like that I had seen in the corridor outside – it should be more oval, with a complexion looking faintly sun-tanned; with a smaller, neater mouth; surrounded by chestnut hair that curled naturally; with brown eyes rather wide apart and perhaps a little grave as a rule.

I knew, too, how the rest of me should look – slender, long-legged, with small, firm breasts – a nice body, but one that I had simply taken for granted until Donald gave me pride in it by loving it. . . .

I looked down at the repulsive mound of pink satin, and shuddered. A sense of outrage came welling up. I longed for Donald to comfort and pet me and love me and tell me it would be all right; that I wasn't as I was seeing myself at all, and that it *really was* a dream. At the same time I was stricken with horror at the thought that he should ever see me gross and obese like this. And then I remembered that Donald would never see me again at all – never any more – and I was wretched and miserable, and the tears trickled down my cheeks again.

The five others just went on looking at me, wide-eyed and wondering. Half an hour passed, still in silence, then the door opened to admit a whole troop of the little women, all in white suits. I saw Hazel look at me, and then at the leader. She seemed about to speak, and then to change her mind. The little women split up, two to a couch. Standing one on each other, they stripped away the coverlet, rolled up their sleeves, and set to work at massage.

At first it was not unpleasant, and quite soothing. One lay back and relaxed. Presently, however, I liked it less: soon I found it offensive.

'Stop that!' I told the one on the right, sharply.

She paused, smiled at me amiably, though a trifle uncertainly, and then continued.

'I said stop it,' I told her, pushing her away.

Her eyes met mine. They were troubled and hurt, although a professional smile still curved her mouth.

'I mean it,' I added, curtly.

She continued to hesitate, and glanced across at her partner on the further side of the bed.

'You, too,' I told the other. 'That'll do.'

She did not even pause in her rhythm. The one on the right plucked a decision and returned. She re-started just what I had stopped. I reached out and pushed her, harder this time. There must have been a lot more muscle in that bolster of an arm than one would have supposed. The shove carried her half across the room, and she tripped and fell.

All movement in the room suddenly ceased. Everybody stared, first at her, and then at me. The pause was brief. They all set to work again. I pushed away the girl on the left, too, though more gently. The other one picked herself up. She was crying and she looked frightened, but she set her jaw doggedly and started to come back.

'You keep away from me, you little horrors,' I told them threateningly.

That checked them. They stood off, and looked miserably at one another. The one with the badge of seniority fussed up.

'What's the trouble, Mother Orchis?' she inquired.

I told her. She looked puzzled.

'But that's quite right,' she expostulated.

'Not for me. I don't like it, and I won't have it,' I replied. She stood awkwardly, at a loss.

Hazel's voice came from the other side of the room:

'Orchis is off her head. She's been telling us the most disgusting things. She's quite mad.'

The little woman turned to regard her, and then looked inquiringly at one of the others. When the girl confirmed with a nod and an expression of distaste she turned back to me, giving me a searching inspection.

'You two go and report,' she told my discomfited masseuses.

They were both crying now, and they went wretchedly down the room together. The one in charge gave me another long thoughtful look, and then followed them.

A few minutes later all the rest had packed-up and gone. The six of us were alone again. It was Hazel who broke the ensuing silence.

'That was a bitchy piece of work. The poor little devils were only doing their job,' she observed.

'If that's their job, I don't like it,' I told her.

'So you just get them a beating, poor things. But I suppose that's the lost memory again. You wouldn't remember that a Servitor who upsets a Mother is beaten, would you?' she added sarcastically.

'Beaten?' I repeated, uneasily.

'Yes, beaten,' she mimicked. 'But you don't care what becomes of them, do you? I don't know what's happened to you while you were away, but whatever it was it seems to have produced a thoroughly nasty result. I never did care for you, Orchis, though the others thought I was wrong. Well, now we all know.'

None of the rest offered any comment. The feeling that they shared her opinion was strong, but luckily I was spared confirmation by the opening of the door.

The senior attendant re-entered with half a dozen small myrmidons, but this time the group was dominated by a handsome woman of about thirty. Her appearance gave me immense relief. She was neither little, nor Amazonian, nor was she huge. Her present company made her look a little over-tall, perhaps, but I judged her at about five-foot-ten; a normal, pleasant-featured young woman with brown hair, cut somewhat short, and a pleated black skirt showing beneath a white overall. The senior attendant was almost trotting to keep up with her longer steps, and was saying something about delusions and 'only back from the Centre today, Doctor'.

The woman stopped beside my couch while the smaller women huddled together, looking at me with some misgiving. She thrust a thermometer into my mouth and held my wrist. Satisfied on both these counts, she inquired:

'Headache? Any other aches or pains?'

'No,' I told her.

She regarded me carefully. I looked back at her.

'What –?' she began.

'She's mad,' Hazel put in from the other side of the room. 'She says she's lost her memory and doesn't know us.'

'She's been talking about horrid, disgusting things,' added one of the others.

'She's got delusions. She thinks she can read and write,' Hazel supplemented.

The doctor smiled at that.

'Do you?' she asked me.

'I don't see why not – but it should be easy enough to prove,' I replied, brusquely.

She looked startled, a little taken aback, then she recovered her tolerant half-smile.

'All right,' she said, humouring me.

She pulled a small note-pad out of her pocket and offered it to me, with a pencil. The pencil felt a little odd in my hand; the fingers did not fall into place readily on it, nevertheless I wrote:

'I'm only too well aware that I have delusions – and that you are part of them.'

Hazel tittered as I handed the pad back.

The doctor's jaw did not actually drop, but her smile came right off. She looked at me very hard indeed. The rest of the room, seeing her expression, went quiet, as though I had performed some startling feat of magic. The doctor turned towards Hazel.

'What sort of things has she been telling you?' she inquired.

Hazel hesitated, then she blurted out:

'Horrible things. She's been talking about two human sexes – just as if we were like the animals. It was disgusting!'

The doctor considered a moment, then she told the senior attendant:

'Better get her along to the sick-bay. I'll examine her there.'

As she walked off there was a rush of little women to fetch a low trolley from the corner to the side of my couch. A dozen hands assisted me on to it, and then wheeled me briskly away.

'Now,' said the doctor grimly, 'let's get down to it. Who told you all this stuff about two human sexes? I want her name.'

We were alone in a small room with a gold-dotted pink

wallpaper. The attendants, after transferring me from the trolley to a couch again, had taken themselves off. The doctor was sitting with a pad on her knee and a pencil at the ready. Her manner was that of an unbluffable inquisitor.

I was not feeling tactful. I told her not to be a fool.

She looked staggered, flushed with anger for a moment, and then took a hold on herself. She went on:

'After you left the Clinic you had your holiday, of course. Now, where did they send you?'

'I don't know,' I replied. 'All I can tell you is what I told the others – that this hallucination, or delusion, or whatever it is, started in that hospital place you call the Centre.'

With resolute patience she said:

'Look here, Orchis. You were perfectly normal when you left here six weeks ago. You went to the Clinic and had your babies in the ordinary way. *But* between then and now somebody has been filling your head with all this rubbish – and teaching you to read and write, as well. Now you are going to tell me who that somebody was. I warn you you won't get away with this loss of memory nonsense with me. If you are able to remember this nauseating stuff you told the others, then you're able to remember where you got it from.'

'Oh, for heaven's sake talk sense,' I told her. She flushed again.

'I can find out from the Clinic where they sent you, and I can find out from the Rest Home who were your chief associates while you were there, but I don't want to waste time following up all your contacts, so I'm asking you to save trouble by telling me now. You might just as well. We don't want to have to *make* you talk,' she concluded, ominously.

I shook my head.

'You're on the wrong track. As far as I am concerned this whole hallucination, including my connexion with this Orchis, began somehow at the Centre – how it happened I can't tell you, and what happened to her before that just isn't there to be remembered.'

She frowned, obviously disturbed.

B

'What hallucination?' she inquired, carefully.

'Why, this fantastic set-up – and you, too.' I waved my hand to include it all. 'This revolting great body, all those little women, everything. Obviously it is all some projection of the subconscious – and the state of my subconscious is worrying me, for it's certainly no wish-fulfilment.'

She went on staring at me, more worried now.

'Who on earth has been telling you about the subconscious and wish-fulfilments?' she asked, uncertainly.

'I don't see why, even in an hallucination, I am expected to be an illiterate moron,' I replied.

'But a Mother doesn't know anything about such things. She doesn't need to.'

'Listen,' I said. 'I've told you, as I've told those poor grotesques in the other room, that I am *not* a Mother. What I am is just an unfortunate M.B. who is having some kind of nightmare.'

'M.B.?' she inquired, vaguely.

'Bachelor of Medicine. I practise medicine,' I told her.

She went on looking at me curiously. Her eyes wandered over my mountainous form, uncertainly.

'You are claiming to be a doctor?' she said, in an odd voice.

'Colloquially – yes,' I agreed.

There was indignation mixed with bewilderment as she protested:

'But this is sheer nonsense! You were brought up and developed to be a Mother. You *are* a Mother. Just look at you!'

'Yes,' I said, bitterly. 'Just look at me!'

There was a pause.

'It seems to me,' I suggested at last, 'that, hallucination or not, we shan't get much further simply by going on accusing one another of talking nonsense. Suppose you explain to me what this place is, and who you think I am. It might jog my memory.'

She countered that. 'Suppose,' she said, 'that first you tell me what you *can* remember. It would give me more idea of what is puzzling you.'

'Very well,' I agreed, and launched upon a potted history of myself as far as I could recollect it – up to the time, that is to say, when Donald's aircraft crashed.

It was foolish of me to fall for that one. Of course, she had no intention of telling me anything. When she had listened to all I had to say, she went away, leaving me impotently furious.

I waited until the place quietened down. The music had been switched off. An attendant had looked in to inquire, with an air of polishing off the day's duties, whether there was anything I wanted, and presently there was nothing to be heard. I let a margin of half an hour elapse, and then struggled to get up – taking it by very easy stages this time. The greatest part of the effort was to get on to my feet from a sitting position, but I managed it at the cost of heavy breathing. Presently I crossed to the door, and found it unfastened. I held it a little open, listening. There was no sound of movement in the corridor, so I pulled it wide open, and set out to discover what I could about the place. All the doors of the rooms were shut. Putting my ear close to them I could hear regular, heavy breathing behind some, but there were no other sounds in the stillness. I kept on, turning several corners, until I recognized the front door ahead of me. I tried the latch, and found that it was neither barred nor bolted. I paused again, listening for some moments, and then pulled it open and stepped outside.

The park-like garden stretched out before me, sharp-shadowed in the moonlight. Through the trees to the right was a glint of water, to the left was a house similar to the one behind me, with not a light showing in any of its windows.

I wondered what to do next. Trapped in this huge carcass, all but helpless in it, there was very little I could do, but I decided to go on and at least find out what I could while I had the chance. I went forward to the edge of the steps that I had earlier climbed from the ambulance, and started down them cautiously, holding on to the balustrade.

'Mother,' said a sharp, incisive voice behind me. 'What are you doing?'

I turned and saw one of the little women, her white suit gleaming in the moonlight. She was alone. I made no reply, but took another step down. I could have wept at the outrage of the heavy, ungainly body, and the caution it imposed on me.

'Come back. Come back at once,' she told me.

I took no notice. She came pattering down after me and laid hold of my draperies.

'Mother,' she said again. 'You must come back. You'll catch cold out here.'

I started to take another step, and she pulled at the draperies to hold me back. I leant forward against the pull. There was a sharp tearing sound as the material gave. I swung round, and lost my balance. The last thing I saw was the rest of the flight of steps coming up to meet me. . . .

As I opened my eyes a voice said:

'That's better, but it was very naughty of you, Mother Orchis. And lucky it wasn't a lot worse. Such a silly thing to do. I'm ashamed of you – really I am.'

My head was aching, and I was exasperated to find that the whole stupid business was still going on; altogether, I was in no mood for reproachful drip. I told her to go to hell. Her small face goggled at me for a moment, and then became icily prim. She applied a piece of lint and plaster to the left side of my forehead, in silence, and then departed, stiffly.

Reluctantly, I had to admit to myself that she was perfectly right. What on earth had I been expecting to do – what on earth *could* I do, encumbered by this horrible mass of flesh? A great surge of loathing for it and a feeling of helpless frustration brought me to the verge of tears again. I longed for my own nice, slim body that pleased me and did what I asked of it. I remembered how Donald had once pointed to a young tree swaying in the wind, and introduced it to me as my twin sister. And only a day or two ago. . . .

Then, suddenly, I made a discovery which brought me struggling to sit up. The blank part of my mind had filled up. I could remember everything. . . . The effort made my head throb, so I relaxed and lay back once more, recalling it all, right up to the point where the needle was withdrawn and someone swabbed my arm. . . .

But what had happened after that? Dreams and hallucinations I had expected . . . but not the sharp-focused, detailed sense of reality . . . not this state which was like a nightmare made solid. . . .

What, what in heaven's name, had they done to me. . . ?

I must have fallen asleep again, for when I opened my eyes there was daylight outside, and a covey of little women had arrived to attend to my toilet.

They spread their sheets dexterously and rolled me this way and that with expert technique as they cleaned me up. I suffered their industry patiently, feeling the fresher for it, and glad to discover that the headache had all but gone.

When we were almost at the end of our ablutions there came a peremptory knock, and without invitation two figures, dressed in black uniforms with silver buttons, entered. They were the Amazon type, tall, broad, well set-up, and handsome. The little women dropped everything and fled with squeaks of dismay into the far corner of the room where they cowered in a huddle.

The two gave me the familiar salute. With an odd mixture of decision and deference one of them inquired:

'You are Orchis – Mother Orchis?'

'That's what they're calling me,' I admitted.

The girl hesitated, then, in a tone rather more pleading than ordering, she said:

'I have orders for your arrest, Mother. You will please come with us.'

An excited, incredulous twittering broke out among the little women in the corner. The uniformed girl quelled them with a look.

'Get the Mother dressed and make her ready,' she commanded.

The little women came out of their corner hesitantly,

directing nervous, propitiatory smiles towards the pair. The second one told them briskly, though not altogether unkindly:

'Come along now. Jump to it.'

They jumped.

I was almost swathed in my pink draperies again when the doctor strode in. She frowned at the two in uniform.

'What's all this? What are you doing here?' she demanded.

The leader of the two explained.

'Arrest!' exclaimed the doctor. 'Arrest a Mother! I never heard such nonsense. What's the charge?'

The uniformed girl said, a little sheepishly:

'She is accused of Reactionism.'

The doctor simply stared at her.

'A Reactionist Mother! What'll you people think of next? Go on, get out, both of you.'

The young woman protested:

'We have our orders, Doctor.'

'Rubbish. There's no authority. Have you ever heard of a Mother being arrested?'

'No, Doctor.'

'Well, you aren't going to make a precedent now. Go on.'

The uniformed girl hesitated unhappily, then an idea occurred to her.

'If you would let me have a signed refusal to surrender the Mother . . . ?' she suggested helpfully.

When the two had departed, quite satisfied with their piece of paper, the doctor looked at the little women gloomily.

'You can't help tattling, you servitors, can you? Anything you happen to hear goes through the lot of you like a fire in a cornfield, and makes trouble all round. Well, if I hear any more of this I shall know where it comes from.' She turned to me. 'And you, Mother Orchis, will in future please restrict yourself to yes-and-no in the hearing of these nattering little pests. I'll see you again shortly. We want to ask you some questions,' she added, and went out, leaving a subdued, industrious silence behind her.

*

She returned just as the tray which had held my gargantuan breakfast was being removed, and not alone. The four women who accompanied her, and looked as normal as herself, were followed by a number of little women lugging in chairs which they arranged beside my couch. When they had departed, the five women, all in white overalls, sat down and regarded me as if I were an exhibit. One appeared to be much the same age as the first doctor, two nearer fifty, and one sixty, or more.

'Now, Mother Orchis,' said the doctor, with an air of opening the proceedings, 'it is quite clear that something highly unusual has taken place. Naturally we are interested to understand just what and, if possible, why. You don't need to worry about those police this morning – it was quite improper of them to come here at all. This is simply an inquiry – a scientific inquiry – to establish what has happened.'

'You can't want to understand more than I do,' I replied. I looked at them, at the room about me, and finally at my massive prone form. 'I am aware that all this must be an hallucination, but what is troubling me most is that I have always supposed that any hallucination must be deficient in at least one dimension – must lack reality to some of the senses. But this does not. I have all my senses, and can use them. Nothing is insubstantial: I am trapped in flesh that is very palpably too, too solid. The only striking deficiency, so far as I can see, is reason – even symbolic reason.'

The four other woman stared at me in astonishment. The doctor gave them a sort of now-perhaps-you'll-believe-me glance, and then turned to me again.

'We'll start with a few questions,' she said.

'Before you begin,' I put in, 'I have something to add to what I told you last night. It has come back to me.'

'Perhaps the knock when you fell,' she suggested, looking at my piece of plaster. 'What were you trying to do?'

I ignored that. 'I think I'd better tell you the missing part – it might help – a bit, anyway.'

'Very well,' she agreed. 'You told me you were – er –

married, and that your – er – husband was killed soon afterwards.' She glanced at the others; their blankness of expression was somehow studious. 'It was the part after that that was missing,' she added.

'Yes,' I said. 'He was a test-pilot,' I explained to them. 'It happened six months after we were married – only one month before his contract was due to expire.

'After that, an aunt took me away for some weeks. I don't suppose I'll ever remember that part very well – I – I wasn't noticing anything very much. . . .

'But then I remember waking up one morning and suddenly seeing things differently, and telling myself that I couldn't go on like that. I knew I must have some work, something that would keep me busy.

'Dr Hellyer, who is in charge of the Wraychester Hospital where I was working before I married, told me he would be glad to have me with them again. So I went back, and worked very hard, so that I did not have much time to think. That would be about eight months ago, now.

'Then one day Dr Hellyer spoke about a drug that a friend of his had succeeded in synthesizing. I don't think he was really asking for volunteers, but I offered to try it out. From what he said it sounded as if the drug might have some quite important properties. It struck me as a chance to do something useful. Sooner or later, someone would try it, and as I didn't have any ties and didn't care very much what happened, anyway, I thought I might as well be the one to try it.'

The spokesman doctor interrupted to ask:

'What was this drug?'

'It's called chuinjuatin,' I told her. 'Do you know it?'

She shook her head. One of the others put in:

'I've heard the name. What is it?'

'It's a narcotic,' I told her. 'The original form is in the leaves of a tree that grows chiefly in the south of Venezuela. The tribe of Indians who live there discovered it somehow, like others did quinine and mescalin. And in much the same way they use it for orgies. Some of them sit and chew the leaves –

they have to chew about six ounces of them – and gradually they go into a zombie-like, trance state. It lasts three or four days during which they are quite helpless and incapable of doing the simplest thing for themselves, so that other members of the tribe are appointed to look after them as if they were children, and to guard them.

'It's necessary to guard them because the Indian belief is that chuinjuatin liberates the spirit from the body, setting it free to wander anywhere in space and time, and the guardian's most important job is to see that no other wandering spirit shall slip into the body while the true owner is away. When the subjects recover they claim to have had wonderful mystical experiences. There seem to be no physical ill effects, and no craving results from it. The mystical experiences, though, are said to be intense, and clearly remembered.

'Dr Hellyer's friend had tested his synthesized chuinjuatin on a number of laboratory animals and worked out the dosage, and tolerances, and that kind of thing, but what he could not tell, of course, was what validity, if any, the reports of the mystical experiences had. Presumably they were the product of the drug's influence on the nervous system – but whether that effect produced a sensation of pleasure, ecstasy, awe, fear, horror, or any of a dozen more, it was impossible to tell without a human guinea-pig. So that was what I volunteered for.'

I stopped. I looked at their serious, puzzled faces, and at the billow of pink satin in front of me.

'In fact,' I added, 'it appears to have produced a combination of the absurd, the incomprehensible, and the grotesque.'

They were earnest women, these, not to be side-tracked. They were there to disprove an anomaly – if they could.

'I see,' said the spokeswoman with an air of preserving reasonableness, rather than meaning anything. She glanced down at a paper on which she had made a note from time to time.

'Now, can you give us the time and date at which this experiment took place?'

I could, and did, and after that the questions went on and on and on. . . .

The least satisfactory part of it from my point of view was that even though my answers caused them to grow more uncertain of themselves as we went on, they did at least get them; whereas when I put a question it was usually evaded, or answered perfunctorily, as an unimportant digression.

They went on steadily, and only broke off when my next meal arrived. Then they went away, leaving me thankfully in peace – but little the wiser. I half expected them to return, but when they did not I fell into a doze from which I was awakened by the incursion of a cluster of the little women, once more. They brought a trolley with them, and in a short time were wheeling me out of the building on it – but not by the way I had arrived. This time we went down a ramp where another, or the same, pink ambulance waited at the bottom. When they had me safely loaded aboard, three of them climbed in, too, to keep me company. They were chattering as they did so, and they kept it up inconsequently, and mostly incomprehensibly, for the whole hour and a half of the journey that ensued.

The countryside differed little from that I had already seen. Once we were outside the gates there were the same tidy fields and standardized farms. The occasional built-up areas were not extensive and consisted of the same types of blocks close by, and we ran on the same, not very good, road surfaces. There were groups of the Amazon types, and, more rarely, individuals, to be seen at work in the fields; the sparse traffic was lorries, large or small, and occasional buses, but with never a private car to be seen. My illusion, I reflected, was remarkably consistent in its details. Not a single group of Amazons, for instance, failed to raise its right hands in friendly, respectful greeting to the pink car.

Once, we crossed a cutting. Looking down from the bridge I thought at first that we were over the dried bed of a canal, but then I noticed a post leaning at a crazy angle among the grass and weeds: most of its attachments had fallen off, but there were enough left to identify it as a railway-signal.

We passed through one concentration of identical blocks which was in size, though in no other way, quite a town, and then, two or three miles farther on, ran through an ornamental gateway into a kind of park.

In one way it was not unlike the estate we had left, for everything was meticulously tended; the lawns like velvet, the flower-beds vivid with spring blossoms, but it differed essentially in that the buildings were not blocks. They were houses, quite small for the most part, and varied in style, often no larger than roomy cottages. The place had a subduing effect on my small companions; for the first time they left off chattering, and gazed about them with obvious awe.

The driver stopped once to inquire the way of an overalled Amazon who was striding along with a hod on her shoulder. She directed us, and gave me a cheerful, respectful grin through the window, and presently we drew up again in front of a neat little two-storey Regency-style house.

This time there was no trolley. The little women, assisted by the driver, fussed over helping me out, and then half-supported me into the house, in a kind of buttressing formation.

Inside, I was manoeuvred with some difficulty through a door on the left, and found myself in a beautiful room, elegantly decorated and furnished in the period-style of the house. A white-haired woman in a purple silk dress was sitting in a wing-chair beside a wood fire. Both her face and her hands told of considerable age, but she looked at me from keen, lively eyes.

'Welcome, my dear,' she said, in a voice which had no trace of the quaver I half-expected.

Her glance went to a chair. Then she looked at me again, and thought better of it.

'I expect you'd be more comfortable on the couch,' she suggested.

I regarded the couch – a genuine Georgian piece, I thought – doubtfully.

'Will it stand it?' I wondered.

'Oh, I think so,' she said, but not too certainly.

The retinue deposited me there carefully, and stood by, with anxious expressions. When it was clear that though it creaked it was probably going to hold, the old lady shooed them away, and rang a little silver bell. A diminutive figure, a perfect parlourmaid three-foot-ten in height, entered.

'The brown sherry, please, Mildred,' instructed the old lady. 'You'll take sherry, my dear?' she added to me.

'Y-yes – yes, thank you,' I said, faintly. After a pause I added: 'You will excuse me, Mrs – er – Miss –?'

'Oh, I should have introduced myself. My name is Laura – not Miss, or Mrs, just Laura. You, I know, are Orchis – Mother Orchis.'

'So they tell me,' I owned, distastefully.

We studied one another. For the first time since the hallucination had set in I saw sympathy, even pity, in someone else's eyes. I looked round the room again, noticing the perfection of details.

'This is – I'm not mad, am I?' I asked.

She shook her head slowly, but before she could reply the miniature parlourmaid returned, bearing a cut-glass decanter and glasses on a silver tray. As she poured out a glass for each of us I saw the old lady glance from her to me and back again, as though comparing us. There was a curious, uninterpretable expression on her face. I made an effort.

'Shouldn't it be Madeira?' I suggested.

She looked surprised, and then smiled, and nodded appreciatively.

'I think you have accomplished the purpose of this visit in one sentence,' she said.

The parlourmaid left, and we raised our glasses. The old lady sipped at hers and then placed it on an occasional table beside her.

'Nevertheless,' she went on, 'we had better go into it a little more. Did they tell you why they have sent you to me, my dear?'

'No,' I shook my head.

'It is because I am an historian,' she informed me. 'Access to history is a privilege. It is not granted to many of us nowadays – and then somewhat reluctantly. Fortunately, a feeling that no branches of knowledge should be allowed to perish entirely still exists – though some of them are pursued at the cost of a certain political suspicion.' She smiled deprecatingly, and then went on. 'So when confirmation is required it is necessary to appeal to a specialist. Did they give you any report on their diagnosis?'

I shook my head again.

'I thought not. So like the profession, isn't it? Well, I'll tell you what they told me on the telephone from the Mothers' Home, and we shall have a better idea of what we are about. I was informed that you have been interviewed by several doctors whom you have interested, puzzled – and I suspect, distressed – very much, poor things. None of them has more than a minimum smattering of history, you see. Well, briefly, two of them are of the opinion that you are suffering from delusions of a schizophrenic nature: and three are inclined to think you are a genuine case of transferred personality. It is an extremely rare condition. There are not more than three reliably documented cases, and one that is more debatable, they tell me; but of those confirmed two are associated with the drug chuinjuatin, and the third with a drug of very similar properties.

'Now, the majority of three found your answers coherent for the most part, and felt that they were authentically circumstantial. That is to say that nothing you told them conflicted directly with what they know, but, since they know so little outside their professional field, they found a great deal of the rest both hard to believe and impossible to check. Therefore I, with my better means of checking, have been asked for my opinion.'

She paused, and looked me thoughtfully over.

'I rather think,' she added, 'that this is going to be one of the most curiously interesting things that has happened to me in my quite long life. – Your glass is empty, my dear.'

'Transferred personality,' I repeated wonderingly, as I held out my glass. 'Now, if *that* were possible –'

'Oh, there's no doubt about the *possibility*. Those three cases I mentioned are fully authenticated.'

'It might be that – almost,' I admitted. 'At least, in some ways it might be – but not in others. There *is* this nightmare quality. *You* seem perfectly normal to me, but look at me, myself – and at your little maid! There's certainly an element of delusion. I *seem* to be here, like this, and talking to you – but it can't really be so, so where am I?'

'I can understand, better than most, I think, how unreal this must seem to you. In fact, I have spent so much of my time in books that it sometimes seems unreal to me – as if I did not quite belong anywhere. Now, tell me my dear, when were you born?'

I told her. She thought for a moment.

'H'm,' she said. 'George the Sixth – but you'd not remember the second big war?'

'No,' I agreed.

'But you might remember the coronation of the next monarch? Whose was that?'

'Elizabeth – Elizabeth the Second. My mother took me to see the procession,' I told her.

'Do you remember anything about it?'

'Not a lot really – except that it rained, nearly all day,' I admitted.

We went on like that for a little while, then she smiled, reassuringly.

'Well, I don't think we need any more to establish our point. I've heard about that coronation before – at second-hand. It must have been a wonderful scene in the abbey.' She mused a moment, and gave a little sigh. 'You've been very patient with me, my dear. It is only fair that you should have your turn – but I'm afraid you must prepare yourself for some shocks.'

'I think I must be inured after my last thirty-six hours – or what has appeared to be thirty-six hours,' I told her.

'I doubt it,' she said, looking at me seriously.

'Tell me,' I asked her. 'Please explain it all – if you can.'

'Your glass, my dear. Then I'll get the crux of it over.' She poured for each of us, then she asked:

'What strikes you as the oddest feature of your experience, so far?'

I considered. 'There's so much –'

'Might it not be that you have not seen a single man?' she suggested.

I thought back. I remembered the wondering tone of one of the Mothers asking: 'What is a man?'

'That's certainly one of them,' I agreed. 'Where are they?'

She shook her head, watching me steadily.

'There aren't any, my dear. Not any more. None at all.'

I simply went on staring at her. Her expression was perfectly serious and sympathetic. There was no trace of guile there, or deception, while I struggled with the idea. At last I managed:

'But – but that's impossible! There must be some somewhere. . . . You couldn't – I mean, how? – I mean. . . .' My expostulation trailed off in confusion.

She shook her head.

'I know it must seem impossible to you, Jane – may I call you Jane? But it is so. I am an old woman now, nearly eighty, and in all my long life I have never seen a man – save in old pictures and photographs. Drink your sherry, my dear. It will do you good.' She paused. 'I'm afraid this upsets you.'

I obeyed, too bewildered for further comment at the moment, protesting inwardly, yet not altogether disbelieving, for certainly I had not seen one man, nor sign of any. She went on quietly, giving me time to collect my wits:

'I can understand a little how you must feel. I haven't had to learn all my history entirely from books, you see. When I was a girl, sixteen or seventeen, I used to listen a lot to my grandmother. She was as old then as I am now, but her memory of her youth was still very good. I was able almost to see the places she talked about – but they were part of such a different world that it was difficult for me to understand how she felt. When she spoke about the young man she had been engaged to, tears would roll down her cheeks, even then – not just for him, of course, but for the whole world that she had known as a girl. I was sorry for her, although I could not really understand how she felt. – How should I? But now that I am old, too, and have read so much, I am perhaps a little nearer to understanding her feelings, I think.' She looked at me curiously. 'And you, my dear. Perhaps you, too, were engaged to be married?'

'I was married – for a little time,' I told her.

She contemplated that for some seconds, then:

'It must be a very strange experience to be owned,' she remarked, reflectively.

'Owned?' I exclaimed, in astonishment.

'Ruled by a husband,' she explained, sympathetically.

I stared at her.

'But it – it wasn't like that – it wasn't like that at all,' I protested. 'It was –' But there I broke off, with tears too close. To sheer her away I asked:

'But what happened? What on earth happened to the men?'

'They all died,' she told me. 'They fell sick. Nobody could do anything for them, so they died. In little more than a year they were all gone – all but a very few.'

'But surely – surely everything would collapse?'

'Oh, yes. Very largely it did. It was very bad. There was a dreadful lot of starvation. The industrial parts were the worst hit, of course. In the more backward countries and in rural areas women were able to turn to the land and till it to keep themselves and their children alive, but almost all the large organizations broke down entirely. Transport ceased very soon: petrol ran out, and no coal was being mined. It was quite a dreadful state of affairs because although there were a great many women, and they had outnumbered the men, in fact, they had only really been important as consumers and spenders of money. So when the crisis came it turned out that scarcely any of them knew how to do any of the important things because they had nearly all been owned by men, and had to lead their lives as pets and parasites.'

I started to protest, but her frail hand waved me aside.

'It wasn't their fault – not entirely,' she explained. 'They were caught up in a process, and everything conspired against their escape. It was a long process, going right back to the eleventh century, in Southern France. The Romantic conception started there as an elegant and amusing fashion for the leisured classes. Gradually, as time went on, it permeated through most levels of society, but it was not until the latter part of the nineteenth century that its commercial possibilities were intelligently perceived, and not until the twentieth that it was really exploited.

'At the beginning of the twentieth century women were starting to have their chance to lead useful, creative, interesting lives. But that did not suit commerce: it needed them much more as mass-consumers than as producers – except on the most routine levels. So Romance was adopted and developed as a weapon against their further progress and to promote consumption, and it was used intensively.

'Women must never for a moment be allowed to forget their sex, and compete as equals. Everything had to have a "feminine angle" which must be different from the masculine angle, and be dinned in without ceasing. It would have been unpopular for manufacturers actually to issue an order "back to the kitchen", but there were other ways. A profession without a difference, called "housewife", could be invented. The kitchen could be glorified and made more expensive; it could be made to seem desirable, and it could be shown that the way to realize this heart's desire was through marriage. So the presses turned out, by the hundred thousand a week, journals which concentrated the attention of women ceaselessly and relentlessly upon selling themselves to some man in order that they might achieve some small, uneconomic unit of a home upon which money could be spent.

'Whole trades adopted the romantic approach and the glamour was spread thicker and thicker in the articles, the write-ups, and most of all in the advertisements. Romance found a place in everything that women might buy from underclothes to motor-cycles, from "health" foods to kitchen stoves, from deodorants to foreign travel, until soon they were too bemused to be amused any more.

'The air was filled with frustrated moanings. Women maundered in front of microphones yearning only to "surrender", and "give themselves", to adore and to be adored. The cinema most of all maintained the propaganda, persuading the main and important part of their audience, which was female, that nothing in life was worth achieving but dewy-eyed passivity in the strong arms of Romance. The pressure became such that the majority of young women spent all their leisure time dreaming of Romance, and the means of securing it. They were brought to a state of honestly believing that to be owned by some man and set down in a little brick box to buy all the things that the manufacturers wanted them to buy would be the highest form of bliss that life could offer.'

'But –' I began to protest again. The old lady was now well launched, however, and swept on without a check.

'All this could not help distorting society, of course. The divorce-rate went up. Real life simply could not come near to providing the degree of romantic glamour which was being represented as every girl's proper inheritance. There was probably, in the aggregate, more disappointment, disillusion, and dissatisfaction among women than there had ever been before. Yet, with this ridiculous and ornamental ideal grained-in by unceasing propaganda, what could a conscientious idealist do but take steps to break up the short-weight marriage she had made, and seek elsewhere for the ideal which was hers, she understood, by right?

'It was a wretched state of affairs brought about by deliberately promoted dissatisfaction; a kind of rat-race with, somewhere safely out of reach, the glamorized romantic ideal always luring. Perhaps an exceptional few almost attained it, but, for all except those very few, it was a cruel, tantalizing sham on which they spent themselves, and of course their money, in vain.'

This time I did get in my protest.

'But it wasn't like that. Some of what you say may be true – but that's all the superficial part. It didn't feel a bit like the way you put it. I was in it. I *know*.'

She shook her head reprovingly.

'There is such a thing as being too close to make a proper evaluation. At a distance we are able to see more clearly. We can perceive it for what it was – a gross and heartless exploitation of the weaker-willed majority. Some women of education and resolution were able to withstand it, of course, but at a cost. There must always be a painful price for resisting majority pressure – even they could not always, altogether escape the feeling that they might be wrong, and that the rat-racers were having the better time of it.

'You see, the great hopes for the emancipation of women with which the century had started had been outflanked. Purchasing-power had passed into the hands of the ill-educated and highly-suggestible. The desire for Romance is essentially a selfish wish, and when it is encouraged to dominate every other it breaks down all corporate loyalties. The individual woman thus separated from, and yet at the same time thrust into competition with, all other women was almost defenceless; she became the prey of organized suggestion. When it was represented to her that the lack of certain goods or amenities would be fatal to Romance she became alarmed and, thus, eminently exploitable. She could only believe what she was told, and spent a great deal of time worrying about whether she was doing all the right things to encourage Romance. Thus, she became, in a new, a subtler way, more exploited, more dependent, and less creative than she had ever been before.'

'Well,' I said, 'this is the most curiously unrecognizable account of my world that I have ever heard – it's like something copied, but with all the proportions wrong. And as for "less creative" – well, perhaps families were smaller, but women still went on having babies. The population was still increasing.'

The old lady's eyes dwelt on me a moment.

'You are undoubtedly a thought-child of your time, in some ways,' she observed. 'What makes you think there is anything creative about having babies? Would you call a plant-pot creative because seeds grow in it? It is a mechanical operation – and, like most mechanical operations, is most easily performed by the least intelligent. Now, bringing up a child, educating, helping her to become a *person*, that *is* creative. But unfortunately, in the time we are speaking of, women had, in the main, been successfully conditioned into bringing up their daughters to be unintelligent consumers, like themselves.'

'But,' I said helplessly, 'I *know* the time. It's my time. This is all distorted.'

'The perspective of history must be truer,' she told me again, unimpressed, and went on: 'But if what happened *had* to happen, then it chose a fortunate time to happen. A hundred years earlier, even fifty years earlier, it would very likely have meant extinction. Fifty years later might easily have been too late – it might have come upon a world in which *all* women had profitably restricted themselves to domesticity and consumership. Luckily, however, in the middle of the century some women were still entering the professions, and by far the greatest number of professional women was to be found in medicine – which is to say that they were only really numerous in, and skilled in, the very profession which immediately became of vital importance if we were to survive at all.

'I have no medical knowledge, so I cannot give you any details of the steps they took. All I can tell you is that there was intensive research on lines which will probably be more obvious to you than they are to me.

'A species, even our species, has great will to survive, and the doctors saw to it that the will had the means of expression. Through all the hunger, and the chaos, and the other priva-tions, babies somehow continued to be born. That had to be.

Reconstruction could wait: the priority was the new generation that would help in the reconstruction, and then inherit it. So babies were born: the girl babies lived, the boy babies died. That was distressing, and wasteful, too, and so, presently, only girl babies were born – again, the means by which that could be achieved will be easier for you to understand than for me.

'It is, they tell me, not nearly so remarkable as it would appear at first sight. The locust, it seems, will continue to produce female locusts without male, or any other kind of assistance, the aphis, too, is able to go on breeding alone and in seclusion, certainly for eight generations, perhaps more. So it would be a poor thing if we, with all our knowledge and powers of research to assist us, should find ourselves inferior to the locust and the aphis in this respect, would it not?'

She paused, looking at me somewhat quizzically for my response. Perhaps she expected amazed – or possibly shocked – disbelief. If so, I disappointed her: technical achievements have ceased to arouse simple wonder since atomic physics showed how the barriers fall before the pressure of a good brains-team. One can take it that most things are possible: whether they are desirable, or worth doing, is a different matter – and one that seemed to me particularly pertinent to her question. I asked her:

'And what is it that you have achieved?'

'Survival,' she said, simply.

'Materially,' I agreed, 'I suppose you have. But when it has cost all the rest, when love, art, poetry, excitement, and physical joy have all been sacrificed to mere continued existence, what is left but a soulless waste? What reason is there any longer for survival?'

'As to the reason, I don't know – except that survival is a desire common to all species. I am quite sure that the *reason* for that desire was no clearer in the twentieth century than it is now. But, for the rest, why should you assume that they are gone? Did not Sappho write poetry? And your assumption that the possession of a soul depends upon a duality of sexes surprises me: it has so often been held that the two are in some sort of conflict, has it not?'

'As an historian who must have studied men, women, and motives you should have taken my meaning better,' I told her.

She shook her head, with reproof. 'You are so much the conditioned product of your age, my dear. They told you, on all levels, from the works of Freud to that of the most nugatory magazines for women, that it was sex, civilized into romantic love, that made the world go round – and you believed them. But the world continues to go round for others, too – for the insects, the fish, the birds, the animals – and how much do you suppose they know of romantic love, even in brief mating-seasons? They hoodwinked you, my dear. Between them they channelled your interests and ambitions along courses that were socially convenient, economically profitable, and almost harmless.'

I shook my head.

'I just don't believe it. Oh, yes, you know something of my world – from the outside. But you don't understand it, or feel it.'

'That's your conditioning, my dear,' she told me, calmly.

Her repeated assumption irritated me. I asked:

'Suppose I were to believe what you say, what is it, then, that *does* make the world go round?'

'That's simple, my dear. It is the will to power. We have that as babies; we have it still in old age. It occurs in men and women alike. It is more fundamental, and more desirable, than sex; I tell you, you were misled – exploited, sublimated for economic convenience.

'After the disease had struck, women ceased, for the first time in history, to be an exploited class. Without male rulers to confuse and divert them they began to perceive that all true power resides in the female principle. The male had served only one brief useful purpose; for the rest of his life he was a painful and costly parasite.

'As they became aware of power, the doctors grasped it.

In twenty years they were in full control. With them were the few women engineers, architects, lawyers, administrators, some teachers, and so on, but it was the doctors who held the keys of life and death. The future was in their hands and, as things began gradually to revive, they, together with the other professions, remained the dominant class and became known as the Doctorate. It assumed authority; it made the laws; it enforced them.

'There was opposition, of course. Neither the memory of the old days, nor the effect of twenty years of lawlessness, could be wiped out at once, but the doctors had the whiphand – any woman who wanted a child had to come to them, and they saw to it that she was satisfactorily settled in a community. The roving gangs dwindled away, and gradually order was restored.

'Later on, they faced better-organized opposition. There was a party which contended that the disease which had struck down the men had run its course, and the balance could, and should, be restored – they were known as Reactionists, and they became an embarrassment.

'Most of the Council of the Doctorate still had clear memories of a system which used every weakness of women, and had been no more than a mere civilized culmination of their exploitation through the ages. They remembered how they themselves had only grudgingly been allowed to qualify for their careers. They were now in command: they felt no obligation to surrender their power and authority, and eventually, no doubt, their freedom to a creature whom they had proved to be biologically, and in all other ways, expendable. They refused unanimously to take a step that would lead to corporate suicide, and the Reactionists were proscribed as a subversive criminal organization.

'That, however, was just a palliative. It quickly became clear that they were attacking a symptom and neglecting the cause. The Council was driven to realize that it had an unbalanced society at its hands – a society that was capable of continuity, but was in structure, you might say, little more than the residue of a vanished form. It could not continue in that truncated shape, and as long as it tried to disaffection would increase. Therefore, if power was to become stable, a new form suitable to the circumstances must be found.

'In deciding the shape it should take, the natural tendencies of the little-educated and uneducated woman were carefully considered – such qualities as her feeling for hierarchical principles and her disposition to respect artificial distinctions. You will no doubt recollect that in your own time any fool of a woman whose husband was ennobled or honoured at once acquired increased respect and envy from other women though she remained the same fool; and also, that any gathering or society of unoccupied women would soon become obsessionally enmeshed in the creation and preservation of social distinctions. Allied to this is the high value they usually place upon a feeling of security. Important, too, is the capacity for devoted self-sacrifice, and slavery to conscience within the canons of any local convention. We are naturally very biddable creatures. Most of us are happiest when we are being orthodox, however odd our customs may appear to an outsider; the difficulty in handling us lies chiefly in establishing the required standards of orthodoxy.

'Obviously, the broad outline of a system which was going to stand any chance of success, would have to provide scope for these and other characteristic traits. It must be a scheme where the interplay of forces would preserve equilibrium and respect for authority. The details of such an organization, however, were less easy to determine.

'An extensive study of social forms and orders was undertaken but for several years every plan put forward was rejected as in some way unsuitable. The architecture of that finally chosen was said, though I do not know with how much truth, to have been inspired by the Bible – a book at that time still unprohibited, and the source of much unrest – I am told that it ran something like: "Go to the ant, thou sluggard; consider her ways."

'The Council appears to have felt that this advice, suitably modified, could be expected to lead to a state of affairs which would provide most of the requisite characteristics.

'A four-class system was chosen as the basis, and strong differentiations were gradually introduced. These, now that they have become well established, greatly help to ensure stability – there is scope for ambition within one's class, but none for passing from one class to another. Thus, we have the Doctorate – the educated ruling-class, fifty per cent of whom are actually of the medical profession. The Mothers, whose title is self-explanatory. The Servitors who are numerous and, for psychological reasons, small. The Workers, who are physically and muscularly strong, to do the heavier work. All the three lower classes respect the authority of the Doctorate. Both the employed classes revere the Mothers. The Servitors consider themselves more favoured in their tasks than the Workers; and the Workers tend to regard the puniness of the Servitors with a semi-affectionate contempt.

'So you see a balance has been struck, and though it works somewhat crudely as yet, no doubt it will improve. It seems likely, for instance, that it would be advant agous to introduce sub-divisions into the Servitor class before long, and the police are thought by some to be put at a disadvantage by having no more than a little education to distinguish them from the ordinary Worker. . . .'

She went on explaining with increasing detail while the enormity of the whole process gradually grew upon me.

'Ants!' I broke in, suddenly. 'The ant-nest! You've taken *that* for your model?'

She looked surprised, either at my tone, or the fact that what she was saying had taken so long to register.

'And why not?' she asked. 'Surely it is one of the most enduring social patterns that nature has evolved – though of course some adaptation –'

'You're – are you telling me that only the Mothers have children?' I demanded.

'Oh, members of the Doctorate do, too, when they wish,' she assured me.

'But – but –'

'The Council decides the ratios,' she went on to explain. 'The doctors at the clinic examine the babies and allocate them suitably to the different classes. After that, of course, it is just a matter of seeing to their specialized feeding, glandular control, and proper training.'

'But,' I objected wildly, 'what's it *for*? Where's the sense in it? What's the good of being alive, like that?'

'Well, what *is* the sense in being alive? You tell me,' she suggested.

'But we're *meant* to love and be loved, to have babies we love by people we love.'

'There's your conditioning again; glorifying and romanticizing primitive animalism. Surely you consider that we are superior to the animals?'

'Of course I do, but –'

'Love, you say, but what can you know of the love there can be between mother and daughter when there are no men to introduce jealousy? Do you know of any purer sentiment than the love of a girl for her little sisters?'

'But you don't understand,' I protested again. 'How should you understand a love that colours the whole world? How it centres in your heart and reaches out from there to pervade your whole being, how it can affect everything you are, everything you touch, everything you hear. . . . It can hurt dreadfully, I know, oh, I know, but it can run like sunlight in your veins. . . . It can make you a garden out of a slum; brocade out of rags; music out of a speaking voice. It can show you a whole universe in someone else's eyes. Oh, you don't understand . . . you don't know . . . you can't. . . . Oh, Donald, darling, how can I show her what she's never even guessed at . . . ?'

There was an uncertain pause, but presently she said:

'Naturally, in your form of society it was necessary for you to be given such a conditioned reaction, but you can scarcely expect us to surrender our freedom, to connive at our own re-subjection, by calling our oppressors into existence again.'

'Oh, you *won't* understand. It was only the more stupid men and women who were continually at war with one another. Lots of us were complementary. We were pairs who formed units.'

She smiled. 'My dear, either you are surprisingly ill-informed on your own period, or else the stupidity you speak of was astonishingly dominant. Neither as myself, nor as an historian, can I consider that we should be justified in resurrecting such a state of affairs. A primitive stage of our development has now given way to a civilized era. Woman, who is the vessel of life, had the misfortune to find man necessary for a time, but now she does no longer. Are you suggesting that such a useless and dangerous encumbrance ought to be preserved, out of sheer sentimentality? I will admit that we have lost some minor conveniences – you will have noticed, I expect, that we are less inventive mechanically, and tend to copy the patterns we have inherited; but that troubles us very little; our interests lie not in the inorganic, but in the organic and the sentient. Perhaps men could show us how to travel twice as fast, or how to fly to the moon, or how to kill more people more quickly; but it does not seem to us that such kinds of knowledge would be good payment for re-enslaving ourselves. No, our kind of world suits us better – all of us except a few Reactionists. You have seen our Servitors. They are a little timid in manner, perhaps, but are they oppressed, or sad? Don't they chatter among themselves as brightly and perkily as sparrows? And the Workers – those you called the Amazons – don't they look strong, healthy, and cheerful?'

'But you're robbing them all – robbing them of their birthright.'

'You mustn't give me cant, my dear. Did not your social system conspire to rob a woman of her "birthright" unless she married? You not only let her know it, but you socially rubbed it in: here, our Servitors and Workers do not know it, and they are not worried by a sense of inadequacy. Motherhood is the function of the Mothers, and understood as such.'

I shook my head. 'Nevertheless, they *are* being robbed. A woman has a right to love –'

For once she was a little impatient as she cut me short.

'You keep repeating to me the propaganda of your age. The love you talk about, my dear, existed in your little sheltered part of the world by polite and profitable convention. You were scarcely ever allowed to see its other face, unglamorized by Romance. *You* were never openly bought and sold, like livestock; *you* never had to sell yourself to the first-comer in order to live; *you* did not happen to be one of the women who through the centuries have screamed in agony and suffered and died under invaders in a sacked city – nor were you ever flung into a pit of fire to be saved from them; *you* were never compelled to suttee upon your dead husband's pyre; *you* did not have to spend your whole life imprisoned in a harem; *you* were never part of the cargo of a slave-ship; *you* never retained your own life only at the pleasure of your lord and master. . . .

'That is the other side – the age-long side. There is going to be no more of such things. They are finished at last. Dare you suggest that we should call them back, to suffer them all again?'

'But most of these things had already gone,' I protested. 'The world was getting better.'

'Was it?' she said. 'I wonder if the women of Berlin thought so when it fell? Was it, indeed? – Or was it on the edge of a new barbarism?'

'But if you can only get rid of evil by throwing out the good too, what is there left?'

'There is a great deal. Man was only a means to an end. We needed him in order to have babies. The rest of his vitality accounted for all the misery in the world. We are a great deal better off without him.'

'So you really consider that you've improved on nature?' I suggested.

'Tcha!' she said, impatient with my tone. 'Civilization *is* improvement on nature. Would you want to live in a cave, and have most of your babies die in infancy?'

'There are some things, some fundamental things –' I began, but she checked me, holding up her hand for silence.

Outside, the long shadows had crept across the lawns. In the evening quiet I could hear a choir of women's voices singing, a little distance away. We listened for some minutes until the song was finished.

'Beautiful!' said the old lady. 'Could angels themselves sing more sweetly! They sound happy enough, don't they? Our own lovely children – two of my granddaughters are there among them. They *are* happy, and they've reason to be happy: they're not growing up into a world where they must gamble on the goodwill of some man to keep them; they'll never need to be servile before a lord and master; they'll never stand in danger of rape and butchery, either. Listen to them!'

Another song had started and came lilting lightly to us out of the dusk.

'Why are you crying?' the old lady asked me as it ended.

'I know it's stupid – I don't really believe any of this is what it seems to be – so I suppose I'm crying for all you would have lost if it were true,' I told her. 'There should be lovers out there under the trees; they should be listening hand in hand to that song while they watch the moon rise. But there are no lovers now, there won't be any more. . . .' I looked back at her.

'Did you ever read the lines: "Full many a flower is born to blush unseen, and waste its sweetness on the desert air?" Can't you feel the forlornness of this world you've made? Do you *really* not understand?' I asked.

'I know you've only seen a little of us, but do *you* not begin to understand what it can be like when women are no longer forced to fight one another for the favours of men?' she countered.

We talked on while the dusk gave way to darkness and the lights of other houses started to twinkle through the trees. Her reading had been wide. It had given her even an affection for some periods of the past, but her approval of her own era was unshaken. She felt no aridity in it. Always it was my 'conditioning' which prevented me from seeing that the golden age of woman had begun at last.

'You cling to too many myths,' she told me. 'You speak of a full life, and your instance is some unfortunate woman hugging her chains in a suburban villa. Full life, fiddlesticks! But it was convenient for the traders that she could be made to think so. A truly full life would be an exceedingly short one, in any form of society.'

And so on . . .

At length, the little parlourmaid reappeared to say that my attendants were ready to leave when it should be convenient. But there was one thing I very much wanted to know before I left. I put the question to the old lady.

'Please tell me. How did it – how could it – happen?'

'Simply by accident, my dear – though it was the kind of accident that was entirely the product of its time. A piece of research which showed unexpected, secondary results, that's all.'

'But how?'

'Rather curiously – almost irrelevantly, you might say. Did you ever hear of a man called Perrigan?'

'Perrigan?' I repeated. 'I don't think so, it's an uncommon name.'

'It became very commonly known indeed,' she assured me. 'Doctor Perrigan was a biologist, and his concern was the extermination of rats – particularly the brown rat, which used to do a great deal of expensive damage.

'His approach to the problem was to find a disease which would attack them fatally. In order to produce it he took as his basis a virus infection often fatal to rabbits – or, rather, a group of virus infections that were highly selective, and also unstable since they were highly liable to mutation. Indeed, there was so much variation in the strains that when infection of rabbits in Australia was tried, it was only at the sixth attempt that it was successful; all the earlier strains died out as the rabbits developed immunity. It was tried in other places, too, though with indifferent success until a still more effective strain was started in France, and ran through the rabbit population of Europe.

'Well, taking some of these viruses as a basis, Perrigan induced new mutations by irradiation and other means, and succeeded in producing a variant that would attack rats. That was not enough, however, and he continued his work until he had a strain that had enough of its ancestral selectivity to attack only the brown rat, and with great virulence.

'In that way he settled the question of a long-standing pest, for there are no brown rats now. But something went amiss. It is still an open question whether the successful virus mutated again, or whether one of his earlier experimental viruses was accidently liberated by escaped "carrier" rats, but that's academic. The important thing is that somehow a strain capable of attacking human beings got loose, and that it was already widely disseminated before it was traced – also, that once it was free, it spread with devastating speed; too fast for any effective steps to be taken to check it.

'The majority of women were found to be immune; and of the ten per cent or so whom it attacked over eighty per cent recovered. Among men, however, there was almost no immunity, and the few recoveries were only partial. A few men were preserved by the most elaborate precautions, but they could not be kept confined for ever, and in the end the virus, which had a remarkable capacity for dormancy, got them, too.'

Inevitably several questions of professional interest occurred to me, but for an answer she shook her head.

'I'm afraid I can't help you there. Possibly the medical people will be willing to explain,' she said, but her expression was doubtful.

I manoeuvred myself into a sitting position on the side of the couch.

'I see,' I said. 'Just an accident – yes, I suppose one could scarcely think of it happening any other way.'

'Unless,' she remarked, 'unless one were to look upon it as divine intervention.'

'Isn't that a little impious?'

'I was thinking of the Death of the Firstborn,' she said, reflectively.

There did not seem to be an immediate answer to that. Instead, I asked:

'Can you honestly tell me that you never have the feeling that you are living in a dreary kind of nightmare?'

'Never,' she said. 'There *was* a nightmare – but it's over now. Listen!'

The voices of the choir, reinforced now by an orchestra, reached us distantly out of the darkened garden. No, they were not dreary: they even sounded almost exultant – but then, poor things, how were they to understand . . . ?

My attendants arrived and helped me to my feet. I thanked the old lady for her patience with me and her kindness. But she shook her head.

'My dear, it is I who am indebted to you. In a short time I have learnt more about the conditioning of women in a mixed society than all my books were able to tell me in the rest of my long life. I hope, my dear, that the doctors will find some way of enabling you to forget it, and live happily here with us.'

At the door I paused and turned, still helpfully shored up by my attendants.

'Laura,' I said, using her name for the first time. 'So many of your arguments are right – yet, over all, you're, oh, so *wrong*. Did you never read of lovers? Did you never, as a girl, sigh for a Romeo who would say: "It is the east, and Laura is the sun!"?'

'I think not. Though I have read the play. A pretty, idealized tale – I wonder how much heartbreak it has given to how many would-be Juliets? But I would set a question against yours, my dear Jane. Did you ever see Goya's cycle of pictures called "The Horrors of War"?'

The pink car did not return me to the 'Home'. Our destination turned out to be a more austere and hospital-like building where I was fussed into bed in a room alone. In the morning, after my massive breakfast, three new doctors visited me. Their manner was more social than professional, and we chatted amiably for half an hour. They had evidently been fully informed on my conversation with the old lady, and they were not averse to answering my questions. Indeed, they found some amusement in many of them, though I found none, for there was nothing consolingly vague in what they told me – it all sounded too disturbingly practicable, once the technique had been worked out. At the end of that time, however, their mood changed. One of them, with an air of getting down to business, said:

'You will understand that you present us with a problem. Your fellow Mothers, of course, are scarcely susceptible to Reactionist disaffection – though you have in quite a short time managed to disgust and bewilder them considerably – but on others less stable your influence might be more serious. It is not just a matter of what you may say; your difference from the rest is implicit in your whole attitude. You cannot help that, and, frankly, we do not see how you, as a woman of education, could possibly adapt yourself to the placid, unthinking acceptance that is expected of a Mother. You would quickly feel frustrated beyond endurance. Furthermore, it is clear that the conditioning you have had under your system prevents you from feeling any goodwill towards ours.'

I took that straight; simply as a judgement without bias. Moreover, I could not dispute it. The prospect of spending the rest of my life in pink, scented, soft-musicked illiteracy, interrupted, one gathered, only by the production of quadruplet daughters at regular intervals, would certainly have me violently unhinged in a very short time.

'And so – what?' I asked. 'Can you reduce this great carcass to normal shape and size?'

She shook her head. 'I imagine not – though I don't know that it has ever been attempted. But even if it were possible, you would be just as much of a misfit in the Doctorate – and far more of a liability as a Reactionist influence.'

I could understand that, too.

'What, then?' I inquired.

She hesitated, then she said gently:

'The only practicable proposal we can make is that you should agree to a hypnotic treatment which will remove your memory.'

As the meaning of that came home to me I had to fight off a rush of panic. After all, I told myself, they were being reasonable with me. I must do my best to respond sensibly. Nevertheless, some minutes must have passed before I answered, unsteadily:

'You are asking me to commit suicide. My mind *is* my memories: they are me. If I lose them I shall die, just as surely as if you were to kill my – this body.'

They did not dispute that. How could they?

There is just one thing that makes my life worth living – knowing that you loved me, my sweet, sweet Donald. It is only in my memory that you live now. If you ever leave there you will die again – and for ever.

'No!' I told them. 'No! No!'

At intervals during the day small servitors staggered in under the weight of my meals. Between their visits I had only my thoughts to occupy me, and they were not good company.

'Frankly,' one of the doctors had put it to me, not un-sympathetically, 'we can see no alternative. For years after it happened the annual figures of mental breakdowns were our greatest worry – even though the women then could keep themselves fully occupied with the tremendous amount of work that had to be done, so many of them could not adjust. And we can't even offer you work.'

I knew that it was a fair warning she was giving me – and I knew that, unless the hallucination which seemed to grow more real all the time could soon be induced to dissolve, I was trapped.

During the long day and the following night I tried my hardest to get back to the objectivity I had managed earlier, but I failed. The whole dialectic was too strong for me now;

my senses too consciously aware of my surroundings; the air of consequence and coherence too convincingly persistent. . . .

When they had let me have twenty-four hours to think it over, the same trio visited me again.

'I think,' I told them, 'that I understand better now. What you are offering me is painless oblivion, in place of a breakdown followed by oblivion – and you see no other choice.'

'We don't,' admitted the spokeswoman, and the other two nodded. 'But, of course, for the hypnosis we shall need your co-operation.'

'I realize that,' I told her, 'and I also see now that in the circumstances it would be obstinately futile to withhold it. So I – I – yes, I'm willing to give it – but on one condition.'

They looked at me questioningly.

'It is this,' I explained, 'that you will try one other course first. I want you to give me an injection of chuinjuatin. I want it in precisely the same strength as I had it before – I can tell you the dose.

'You see, whether this is an intense hallucination, or whether it is some kind of projection which makes it seem very similar, it must have something to do with that drug. I'm sure it must – nothing remotely like this has ever happened to me before. So, I thought that if I could repeat the condition – or, would you say believe myself to be repeating the condition? – there may be just a chance . . . I don't know. It may be simply silly . . . but even if nothing comes of it, it can't make things worse in any way now, can it? So, will you let me try it. . . ?'

The three of them considered for some moments.

'I can see no reason why not . . .' said one.

The spokeswoman nodded.

'I shouldn't think there'll be any difficulty with authorization in the circumstances,' she agreed. 'If you want to try, well, it's fair to let you, but – I'd not count on it too much. . . .'

In the afternoon half a dozen small servitors arrived, bustling round, making me and the room ready, with anxious industry. Presently there came one more, scarcely tall enough to see over the trolley of bottles, trays and phials which she pushed to my bedside.

The three doctors entered together. One of the little servitors began rolling up my sleeve. The doctor who had done most of the talking looked at me, kindly, but seriously.

'This is a sheer gamble, you know that?' she said.

'I know. But it's my only chance. I'm willing to take it.'

She nodded, picked up the syringe, and charged it while the little servitor swabbed my monstrous arm. She approached the bedside, and hesitated.

'Go on,' I told her. 'What is there for me here, anyway?'

She nodded, and pressed in the needle. . . .

Now, I have written the foregoing for a purpose. I shall deposit it with my bank, where it will remain unread unless it should be needed.

I have spoken of it to no one. The report on the effect of chuinjuatin – the one that I made to Dr Hellyer where I described my sensation as simply one of floating in space – was false. The foregoing was my true experience.

I concealed it because after I came round, when I found that I was back in my own body in my normal world, the experience haunted me as vividly as if it had been actuality. The details were too sharp, too vivid, for me to get them out of my mind. It overhung me all the time, like a threat. It would not leave me alone. . . .

I did not dare to tell Dr Hellyer how it worried me – he would have put me under treatment. If my other friends did not take it seriously enough to recommend treatment, too, then they would have laughed over it, and amused themselves at my expense interpreting the symbolism. So I kept it to myself.

As I went over parts of it again and again in detail, I grew angry with myself for not asking the old lady for more facts, things like dates, and details that could be verified. If, for instance, the thing should, by her account, have started two or three years ago, then the whole sense of threat would fall to pieces: it would all be discredited. But it had not occurred to me to ask that crucial question. . . . And then, as I went on thinking about it, I remembered that there was one, just one, piece of information that I could check, and I made inquiries. I wish now that I had not, but I felt forced to. . . .

So I have discovered that:

There *is* a Dr Perrigan, he *is* a biologist, he *does* work with rabbits and rats. . . .

He is quite well known in his field. He has published papers on pest-control in a number of journals. It is no secret that he is evolving new strains of myxomatosis intended to attack rats; indeed, he has already developed a group of them and calls them mucosimorbus, though he has not yet succeeded in making them either stable or selective enough for general use. . . .

But I had never heard of this man or his work until his name was mentioned by the old lady in my 'hallucination'. . . .

I have given a great deal of thought to this whole matter. What sort of experience is it that I have recorded above? If it should be a kind of pre-vision of an inevitable, predestined future, then nothing anyone could do would change it. But that does not seem to me to make sense: it is what has happened, and is happening now, that determines the future. Therefore, there must be a great number of *possible* futures, each a possible consequence of what is being done now. It seems to me that under chuinjuatin I saw *one* of those futures. . . .

It was, I think, a warning of what *may* happen – unless it is prevented. . . .

The whole idea is so repulsive, so misconceived, it amounts to such a monstrous aberration of the normal course, that failure to heed the warning would be neglect of duty to one's kind.

I shall, therefore, on my own responsibility and without taking any other person into my confidence, do my best to ensure that such a state as I have described *cannot* come about.

Should it happen that any other person is unjustly accused

of doing, or of assisting me to do, what I intend to do, this
document must stand in his defence. That is why I have
written it.

It is my own unaided decision that Dr Perrigan must not be
permitted to continue his work.

(Signed) JANE WATERLEIGH.

The solicitor stared at the signature for some moments; then
he nodded.

'And so,' he said, 'she then took her car and drove over to
Perrigan's – with this tragic result.'

'From the little I do know of her, I'd say that she probably
did her best to persuade him to give up his work – though she
can scarcely have expected any success with that. It is difficult
to imagine a man who would be willing to give up the work of
years on account of what must sound to him like a sort of
gipsy's warning. So, clearly, she went there prepared to fall
back on direct action, if necessary. It looks as if the police are
quite right when they suppose her to have shot him deliberately;
but not so right when they suppose that she burnt the place
down to hide evidence of the crime. The statement makes it
pretty obvious that her main intention in doing that was to
wipe out Perrigan's work.'

He shook his head. 'Poor girl! There's a clear conviction of
duty in her last page or two: the sort of simplified clarity that
drives martyrs on, regardless of consequences. She has never
denied that she did it. What she wouldn't tell the police is *why*
she did it.'

He paused again, before he added: 'Anyway, thank goodness
for this document. It ought at least to save her life. I should
be very surprised indeed if a plea of insanity could fail, backed
up by this.' He tapped the pile of manuscript with his finger.
'It's a lucky thing she put off her intention of taking it to her
bank.'

Dr Hellyer's face was lined and worried.

'I blame myself most bitterly for the whole thing,' he said.
'I ought never to have let her try the damned drug in the first

place, but I thought she was over the shock of her husband's death. She was trying to keep her time fully occupied, and she was anxious to volunteer. You've met her enough to know how purposeful she can be. She saw it as a chance to contribute something to medical knowledge – which it was, of course. But I ought to have been more careful, and I ought to have seen afterwards that there was something wrong. The real responsibility for this thing runs right back to me.'

'H'm,' said the solicitor. 'Putting that forward as a main line of defence isn't going to do you a lot of good professionally, you know, Hellyer.'

'Possibly not. I can look after that when we come to it. The point is that I hold a responsibility for her as a member of my staff, if for no other reason. It can't be denied that if I had refused her offer to take part in the experiment, this would not have happened. Therefore it seems to me that we ought to be able to argue a state of temporary insanity; that the balance of her mind was disturbed by the effects of the drug which I administered. And if we can get that as a verdict it will result in detention at a mental hospital for observation and treatment – perhaps quite a short spell of treatment.'

'I can't say. We can certainly put it up to counsel and see what he thinks of it.'

'It's valid, too,' Hellyer persisted. 'People like Jane don't do murder if they are in their right minds, not unless they're really in a corner, then they do it more cleverly. Certainly they don't murder perfect strangers. Clearly, the drug caused an hallucination sufficiently vivid to confuse her to a point where she was unable to make a proper distinction between the actual and the hypothetical. She got into a state where she believed the mirage was real, and acted accordingly.'

'Yes. Yes, I suppose one might put it that way,' agreed the solicitor. He looked down again at the pile of paper before him. 'The whole account is, of course, unreasonable,' he said, 'and yet it is pervaded throughout with such an air of reasonableness. I wonder. . . .' He paused pensively, and went on: 'This expendability of the male, Hellyer. She doesn't seem to find it so much incredible, as undesirable. That seems odd in itself to a layman who takes the natural order for granted, but would you, as a medical scientist, say it was – well, not impossible, in theory?'

Dr Hellyer frowned.

'That's very much the kind of question one wants more notice of. It would be very rash to proclaim it *impossible*. Considering it purely as an abstract problem, I can see two or three lines of approach. . . . Of course, if an utterly improbable situation were to arise calling for intensive research – research, that is, on the sort of scale they tackled the atom – well, who can tell . . . ?' He shrugged.

The solicitor nodded again.

'That's just what I was getting at,' he observed. 'Basically it is only just such a little way off the beam; quite near enough to possibility to be faintly disturbing. Mind you, as far as the defence is concerned, her air of thorough conviction, taken in conjunction with the near-plausibility of the thing will probably help. But, for my part, it is just that nearness that is enough to make me a trifle uneasy.'

The doctor looked at him rather sharply.

'Oh, come! Really now! A hardboiled solicitor, too! Don't tell me you're going in for fantasy-building. Anyway, if you are, you'll have to conjure up another one. If Jane, poor girl, has settled one thing, it is that there's no future in this particular fantasy. Perrigan's finished with, and all his work's gone up in smoke and fire.'

'H'm,' said the solicitor, again. 'All the same, it would be more satisfactory if we knew of some way other than this' – he tapped the pile of papers – 'some other way in which she is likely to have acquired some knowledge of Perrigan and his work. There is, as far as one knows, *no* other way in which he can have come into her orbit at all – unless, perhaps, she takes an interest in veterinary subjects?'

'She doesn't. I'm sure of that,' Hellyer told him, shaking his head.

'Well that, then, remains one slightly disturbing aspect. –

'And there is another. You'll think it foolish of me, I'm sure – and no doubt time will prove you right to do so – but I have to admit I'd be feeling just a bit easier in my mind if Jane had been just a bit more thorough in her inquiries before she went into action.'

'Meaning –?' asked Dr Hellyer, looking puzzled.

'Only that she does not seem to have found out that there is a son. But there is, you see. He appears to have taken quite a close interest in his father's work, and is determined that it shan't be wasted. In fact he has already announced that he will do his best to carry it on with the very few specimens that were saved from the fire. . . .

'Laudably filial, no doubt. All the same it does disturb me a little to find that he, also, happens to be a D.Sc., a bio-chemist; and that, very naturally, his name, too, is Perrigan. . . .'

Odd

When, on a day in the late December of 1958, Mr Reginald Aster called upon the legal firm of Cropthorne, Daggit, and Howe, of Bedford Row, at their invitation, he found himself received by a Mr Fratton, an amiable young man, barely out of his twenties, but now head of the firm in succession to the defunct Messrs C, D & H.

And when Mr Aster was informed by Mr Fratton that under the terms of the late Sir Andrew Vincell's will he was a beneficiary to the extent of six thousand Ordinary Shares in British Vinvinyl, Ltd, Mr Aster appeared, as Mr Fratton expressed it to a colleague later, to miss for a while on several plugs.

The relevant clause added that the bequest was made 'in recognition of a most valuable service which he once rendered me'. The nature of this service was not specified, nor was it any of Mr Fratton's business to inquire into it, but the veil over his curiosity was scarcely opaque.

The windfall, standing just then at 83s. 6d. per share, came at a fortunate moment in Mr Aster's affairs. Realization of a small part of the shares enabled him to settle one or two pressing problems, and in the course of this re-ordering, the two men met several times. At length there came a time when Mr Fratton, urged on by curiosity, stepped slightly closer to the edge of professional discretion than he usually permitted himself, to remark in a tentative fashion:

'You did not know Sir Andrew very well, did you?'

It was the kind of advance that Mr Aster could easily have discouraged had he wished to, but, in fact, he made no attempt at parry. Instead, he looked thoughtful, and eyed Mr Fratton with speculation.

'I met Sir Andrew once,' he said. 'For perhaps an hour and a half.'

'That is rather what I thought,' said Mr Fratton, allowing his perplexity to become a little more evident. 'Some time last June, wasn't it?'

'The twenty-fifth of June,' Mr Aster agreed.

'But never before that?'

'No – nor since.'

Mr Fratton shook his head uncomprehendingly.

After a pause Mr Aster said:

'You know, there's something pretty rum about this.'

Mr Fratton nodded, but made no comment. Aster went on:

'I'd rather like to – well, look here, are you free for dinner tomorrow?'

Mr Fratton was, and when the dinner was finished they retired to a quiet corner of the club lounge with coffee and cigars. After a few moments of consideration Aster said:

'I must admit I'd feel happier if this Vincell business was a bit clearer. I don't see – well, there's something altogether off-beat about it. I might as well tell you the whole thing. Here's what happened.'

The twenty-fifth of June was a pleasant evening in an unpleasant summer. I was just strolling home enjoying it. In no hurry at all, and just wondering whether I would turn in for a drink somewhere when I saw this old man. He was standing on the pavement in Thanet Street, holding on to the railings with one hand, and looking about him in a dazed, glassy-eyed way.

Well, in our part of London, as you know, there are plenty of strangers from all over the world, particularly in the summer, and quite a few of them look a bit lost. But this old man – well on in the seventies, I judged – was not that sort. Certainly no tourist. In fact, elegant was the word that occurred to me when I saw him. He had a grey, pointed beard, carefully trimmed, a black felt hat meticulously brushed; a dark suit of excellent cloth and cut; his shoes were expensive; so was his discreetly beautiful silk tie. Gentlemen of this type are not altogether unknown to us in our parts, but they are likely to be off their usual beat; and alone, and in a glassy-eyed condition in public, they are quite rare. One or two people walking ahead of me glanced at him briefly, had the reflex thought about his condition, and passed on. I did not; he did not appear to me to be ordinarily fuddled – more, indeed, as if he were frightened. . . . So I paused beside him.

'Are you unwell?' I asked him. 'Would you like me to call a taxi?'

He turned to look at me. His eyes were bewildered, but it was an intelligent face, slightly ascetic, and made to look the thinner by bushy white eyebrows. He seemed to bring me into focus only slowly; his response came more slowly still, and with an effort.

'No,' he said, uncertainly, 'no, thank you. I – I am not unwell.'

It did not appear to be the full truth, but neither was it a definite dismissal, and, having made the approach, I did not care to leave him like that.

'You have had a shock,' I told him.

His eyes were on the traffic in the street. He nodded, but said nothing.

'There is a hospital just a couple of streets away –' I began. But he shook his head.

'No,' he said again. 'I shall be all right in a minute or two.'

He still did not tell me to go away, and I had a feeling that he did not want me to. His eyes turned this way and that, and then down at himself. At that, he became quite still and tense, staring down at his clothes with an astonishment that could not be anything but real. He let go of the railings, lifted his arm to look at his sleeve, then he noticed his hand – a shapely, well-kept hand, but thin with age, knuckles withered, blue veins prominent. It wore a gold signet ring on the little finger. . . .

Well, we have all read of eyes bulging, but that is the only time I have seen it happen. They looked ready to pop out, and the extended hand began to shake distressingly. He tried to speak, but nothing came. I began to fear that he might be in for a heart attack.

'The hospital –' I began again, but once more he shook his head.

I did not know quite what to do, but I thought he ought to sit down; and brandy often helps, too. He said neither yes nor no to my suggestion, but came with me acquiescently across the street and into the Wilburn Hotel. I steered him to a table in the bar there, and sent for double brandies for both of us. When I turned back from the waiter, the old man was staring across the room with an expression of horror. I looked over there quickly. It was himself he was staring at, in a mirror.

He watched himself intently as he took off his hat and put it down on a chair beside him; then he put up his hand, still trembling, to touch first his beard, and then his handsome silver hair. After that, he sat quite still, staring.

I was relieved when the drinks came. So, evidently, was he. He took just a little soda with his, and then drank the lot. Presently his hand grew steadier, a little colour came into his cheeks, but he continued to stare ahead. Then with a sudden air of resolution he got up.

'Excuse me a moment,' he said, politely.

He crossed the room. For fully two minutes he stood studying himself at short range in the glass. Then he turned and came back. Though not assured, he had an air of more decision, and he signed to the waiter, pointing to our glasses. Looking at me curiously, he said as he sat down again:

'I owe you an apology. You have been extremely kind.'

'Not at all,' I assured him. 'I'm glad to be of any help. Obviously you must have had a nasty shock of some sort.'

'Er – several shocks,' he admitted, and added: 'It is curious how real the figments of a dream can seem when one is taken unaware by them.'

There did not seem to be any useful response to that, so I attempted none.

'Quite unnerving at first,' he added, with a kind of forced brightness.

'What happened?' I asked, feeling still at sea.

'My own fault, entirely my own fault – but I was in a hurry,' he explained. 'I started to cross the road behind a tram, then I saw the one coming in the opposite direction, almost on top of me. I can only think it must have hit me.'

'Oh,' I said, 'er – oh, indeed. Er – where did this happen?'

'Just outside here, in Thanet Street,' he told me.

'You – you don't seem to be hurt,' I remarked.

'Not exactly,' he agreed, doubtfully. 'No, I don't seem to be hurt.'

He did not, nor even ruffled. His clothing was, as I have said, immaculate – besides, they tore up the tram rails in Thanet Street about twenty-five years ago. I wondered if I should tell him that, and decided to postpone it. The waiter brought our glasses. The old man felt in his waistcoat pocket, and then looked down in consternation.

'My sovereign-case! My watch. . . !' he exclaimed.

I dealt with the waiter by handing him a one-pound note. The old man watched intently. When the waiter had given me my change and left:

'If you will excuse me,' I said, 'I think this shock must have caused you a lapse of memory. You do – er – you do remember who you are?'

With his finger still in his waistcoat pocket, and a trace of suspicion in his eyes, he looked at me hard.

'Who I am? Of course I do. I am Andrew Vincell. I live quite close here, in Hart Street.'

I hesitated, then I said:

'There *was* a Hart Street near here. But they changed the name – in the thirties I think; before the war, anyway.'

The superficial confidence which he had summoned up deserted him, and he sat quite still for some moments. Then he felt in the inside pocket of his jacket, and pulled out a wallet. It was made of fine leather, had gold corners, and was stamped with the initials A.V. He eyed it curiously as he laid it on the table. Then he opened it. From the left side he pulled a one-pound note, and frowned at it in a puzzled way; then a five-pound note, which seemed to puzzle him still more.

Without comment he felt in the pocket again, and brought out a slender book clearly intended to pair with the wallet. It, too, bore the initials A.V. in the lower right-hand corner, and in the upper it was stamped simply: 'Diary – 1958.' He held it in his hand, looking at it for quite some time before he lifted his eyes to mine.

'Nineteen-fifty-eight?' he said, unsteadily.

'Yes,' I told him.

There was a long pause, then:

'I don't understand,' he said, almost like a child. 'My life! What has happened to my life?'

His face had a pathetic, crumpled look. I pushed the glass towards him, and he drank a little of the brandy. Opening the diary, he looked at the calendar inside.

'Oh, God!' he said. 'This is too real. What – what has happened to me?'

I said, sympathetically:

'A partial loss of memory isn't unusual after a shock, you know – in a little time it comes back quite all right as a rule. I suggest you look in there' – I pointed to the wallet – 'very likely there will be something to remind you.'

He hesitated, but then felt in the right-hand side of it. The first thing he pulled out was a colour-print of a snapshot; obviously a family group. The central figure was himself, five or six years younger, in a tweed suit; another man, about forty-five, bore a family resemblance, and there were two slightly younger women, and two girls and two boys in their early teens. In the background part of an eighteenth-century house was visible across a well-kept lawn.

'I don't think you need to worry about your life,' I said. 'It would appear to have been very satisfactory.'

There followed three engraved cards, separated by tissues, which announced simply: 'Sir Andrew Vincell', but gave no address. There was also an envelope addressed to Sir Andrew

Vincell, O.B.E., British Vinvinyl Plastics, Ltd, somewhere in London EC1.

He shook his head, took another sip of the brandy, looked at the envelope again, and gave an unamused laugh. Then with a visible effort he took a grip on himself, and said, decisively:

'This is some silly kind of dream. How does one wake up?' He closed his eyes, and declared in a firm tone: 'I am Andrew Vincell. I am aged twenty-three. I live at number forty-eight Hart Street. I am articled to Penberthy and Trull, chartered accountants, of one hundred and two, Bloomsbury Square. This is July the twelfth, nineteen hundred and six. This morning I was struck by a tram in Thanet Street. I must have been knocked silly, and have been suffering from hallucinations. Now!'

He re-opened his eyes, and looked genuinely surprised to find me still there. Then he glared at the envelope, and his expression grew peevish.

'*Sir* Andrew Vincell!' he exclaimed scornfully, 'and Vinvinyl Plastics, Limited! What the devil is that supposed to mean?'

'Don't you think,' I suggested, 'that we must assume that you are a member of the firm – I would say, from appearances, one of its directors?'

'But I told you –' He broke off. 'What *is* plastics?' he went on. 'It doesn't suggest anything but modelling clay to me. What on earth would I be doing with modelling clay?'

I hesitated. It looked as if the shock, whatever it was, had had the effect of cutting some fifty years out of his memory. Perhaps, I thought, if we were to talk of a matter which was obviously familiar and important to him it might stir his recollection. I tapped the table top.

'Well, this, for instance, is a plastic,' I told him.

He examined it, and clicked his finger-nails on it.

'I'd not call that plastic. It is very hard,' he observed.

I tried to explain:

'It was plastic before it hardened. There are lots of different kinds of plastics. This ash-tray, the covering on your chair, this pen, my cheque-book cover, that woman's raincoat, her handbag, the handle of her umbrella, dozens of things all round you – even my shirt is a woven plastic.'

He did not reply immediately, but sat looking from one to another of these things with growing attention. At last he turned back to me again. This time his eyes gazed into mine with great intensity. His voice shook slightly as he said once more:

'This really *is* 1958?'

'Certainly it is,' I assured him. 'If you don't believe your own diary, there's a calendar hanging behind the bar.'

'No horses,' he murmured to himself, 'and the trees in the Square grown so tall . . . a dream is never consistent, not to that extent. . . .' He paused, then, suddenly: 'My God!' he exclaimed, 'my God, if it really *is*. . . .' He turned to me again, with an eager gleam in his eyes. 'Tell me about these plastics,' he demanded urgently.

I am no chemist, and I know no more about them than the next man. However, he was obviously keen, and, as I have said, I thought that a familiar subject might help to revive his memory, so I decided to try. I pointed to the ash-tray.

'Well, this is very likely Bakelite, I think. If so, it is one of the earliest of the thermosetting plastics. A man called Baekeland patented it, about 1909, I fancy. Something to do with phenol and formaldehyde.'

'Thermosetting? What's that?' he inquired.

I did my best with that, and then went on to explain what little I had picked up about molecular chains and arrangements, polymerization and so on, and some of the characteristics and uses. He did not give me any feeling of trying to teach my grandmother, on the contrary, he listened with concentrated attention, occasionally repeating a word now and then as if to fix it in his mind. This hanging upon my words was quite flattering, but I could not delude myself that they were doing anything to revive his memory.

We must – at least, I must – have talked for nearly an hour, and all the time he sat earnest and tense, with his hands clenched tightly together. Then I noticed that the effect of the brandy had worn off, and he was again looking far from well.

'I really think I had better see you home,' I told him. 'Can you remember where you live?'

'Forty-eight Hart Street,' he said.

'No. I mean where you live now,' I insisted.

But he was not really listening. His face still had the expression of great concentration.

'If only I can remember – if only I can remember when I wake up,' he murmured desperately, to himself rather than to me. Then he turned to look at me again.

'What is your name?' he asked.

I told him.

'I'll remember that, too, if I can,' he assured me, very seriously.

I leaned over and lifted the cover of the diary. His name was on the fly-leaf, with an address in Upper Grosvenor Street. I folded the wallet and the diary together, and put them into his hand. He stowed them away in his pocket automatically, and then sat gazing with complete detachment while the porter got us a taxi.

An elderly woman, a housekeeper, I imagine, opened the door of an impressive flat. I suggested that she should ring up Sir Andrew's doctor, and stayed long enough to explain the situation to him when he arrived.

The following evening I rang up to inquire how he was. A younger woman's voice answered. She told me that he had slept well after a sedative, woken somewhat tired, but quite himself, with no sign of any lapse of memory. The doctor saw no cause for alarm. She thanked me for taking care of him, and bringing him home, and that was that.

In fact, I had practically forgotten the whole incident until I saw the announcement of his death in the paper, in December.

Mr Fratton made no comment for some moments, then he drew at his cigar, sipped some coffee, and said, not very constructively:

'It's odd.'

'So I thought – think,' said Mr Aster.

'I mean,' went on Mr Fratton, 'I mean, you certainly did him a kindly service, but scarcely, if you will forgive me, a service that one would expect to find valued at six thousand one-pound shares – standing at eighty-three and sixpence, too.'

'Quite,' agreed Mr Aster.

'Odder still,' Mr Fratton went on, 'this meeting occurred last summer. But the will containing the bequest was drawn up and signed seven years ago.' He again drew thoughtfully on his cigar. 'And I cannot see that I am breaking any confidence if I tell you that it superseded an earlier will drawn up twelve years before, and in that will also, the same clause occurred.' He meditated upon his companion.

'I have given it up,' said Mr Aster, 'but if you are collecting oddities, you might perhaps like to make a note of this one.' He produced a pocket-book, and took from it a cutting. The strip of paper was headed: 'Obituary. Sir Andrew Vincell – A Pioneer in Plastics.' Mr Aster located a passage halfway down the column, and read out:

'"It is curious to note that in his youth Sir Andrew foreshadowed none of his later interests, and was indeed articled at one time to a firm of chartered accountants. At the age of twenty-three, however, in the summer of 1906, he abruptly and quite unexpectedly broke his articles, and began to devote himself to chemistry. Within a few years he had made the first of the important discoveries upon which his great company was subsequently built."'

'H'm,' said Mr Fratton. He looked carefully at Mr Aster. 'He *was* knocked down by a tram in Thanet Street, in 1906 you know.'

'Of course. He told me so,' said Mr Aster.

Mr Fratton shook his head.

'It's all very queer,' he observed.

'Very odd indeed,' agreed Mr Aster.

Oh, Where, Now, is Peggy MacRafferty?

'Oh, where –' is the question they ask in the little grey cottage that rests on the emerald grass of Barranacleugh where the Slieve Gamph sweep down to the bog, 'Oh, where is our Peg? Where is her that was pretty as the ox-eye by the marsh, with her eyes like turf-pools, and her cheeks like Father O'Cracigan's peonies, an' all the sweet, winnin' ways of her? Many a letter have we written to her since she went away, but never a one of them has she answered because we do not know where to send them. Ochone!'

And this was the way it happened.

A letter came to the cottage, addressed to Miss Margaret MacRafferty, and after the postman had reminded her that that was the elegant way of spelling Peggy, she accepted it – and with some excitement, for she had never had a letter of her private own before. When Michael in Canada, Patrick in America, Kathleen in Australia, and Brigit in Liverpool did get to writing, they always addressed it to all MacRaffertys, to save work.

Besides, it was done on a typewriter. She admired it for some time before Eileen said, impatiently:

'Who's it from?'

'How can I tell? I've not opened it,' said Peggy.

'That's what I meant,' said Eileen.

When it was opened, it revealed not only a letter, but a postal order for twenty shillings. After she had studied this, Peggy read the letter carefully, beginning at the top where was printed, Popular Amalgamated Television, Ltd, and continuing steadily to the signature.

'Well, what does it say?' Eileen demanded.

'A man wants to ask me some questions,' Peggy told her.

'Police?' exclaimed her mother, suddenly. 'What've you been doing? Here, let me see.'

They had it sorted out after a while. Somebody, it was not quite clear who, had suggested to the writer that Miss Margaret MacRafferty might be willing to take part in a quiz, with valuable prizes offered. This event would take place in the Town Hall at Ballyloughrish. The writer hoped she would be able to attend, and would supply further details when he received her reply. In the meanwhile he begged to enclose £1 on account of expenses.

'But the bus fare to Ballyloughrish is only three-and-sixpence,' said Peggy, troubled.

'Well you can give him the rest back when you see him,' Eileen pointed out. 'Or at least,' she added, more practically, 'you can give him something. Two shillings, maybe.'

'But suppose I can't answer the questions,' Peggy demurred.

'Oh, for goodness sake! What does that matter? The fare is three-and-six, you give him back two shillings to look right, and threepence for the stamp when you write, that's five and nine, so you get fourteen and threepence just for sitting in the bus to Ballyloughrish and back.'

'But I don't like TV,' objected Peggy. 'Now if it were to do with movies. . . .'

'Oh, you and your movies. Regular old-fashioned you are. A TV personality's what you want to be nowadays.'

'I don't,' said Peggy. 'It's the movies I want to get on.'

'Well, you've got to be seen, haven't you? You've got to start somewhere,' Eileen told her.

So Peggy wrote her acceptance.

But it turned out that there was more to the occasion than just the questions. First there was a kind of high tea at the Ballyloughrish Castle Hotel, with a young Irishman who was something to do with it all, being helpful and nice to her on her right, and another young man on her left who was trying to be just as helpful and nice, but finding it harder because he was an Englishman. Afterwards they went along together to the

Town Hall which was cluttered up with wires, and cameras, and blinding lights, as well as with the whole population of Ballyloughrish.

Luckily they did not begin with Peggy, and she listened carefully to the questions put to her predecessors. They were not nearly as fearsome as she had expected – in fact, the first was always very easy, the second not quite so easy, and the third a little harder, and as those people who didn't fail on the first were failing on the second, she felt quite cheered up. At last her own turn arrived, and she took her place in the box.

Mr Hassop, the question-master, smiled at her.

'Miss Peggy MacRafferty. Well, now, Peggy, it's been your luck to draw the geographical section, so I hope you were good at geography at school, Peggy.'

'Not very,' said Peggy, which for some reason appeared to please the audience.

After some patter Mr Hassop arrived at his first question.

'How many counties of this fair land of yours are still groaning under the foreign yoke, and what are their names?'

Well, that was easy, anyway. The audience applauded.

'Now then, we move across the water to England. I want you to name me five university cities in England.'

She did extra well with that as it had not occurred to her that Oxford-and-Cambridge were separate places, and so had one to spare.

'And now to America . . .'

Peggy was relieved to hear it was America. Partly because Hollywood was in America, and also because as well as her brother Patrick who made automobiles in Detroit, she had two uncles in the New York Police Force, one in the Boston Police Force, one who had been shot in Chicago in the good old days, and one who lived at a place called San Quentin. So she had always taken quite an interest in America, and listened attentively to the question.

'The United States,' said Mr Hassop, 'is, as you know, and as its name tells us, not a single country but a union of states. Now I am not going to ask you to name them all, ha, ha! But what I want you to tell me is how many States go to make up this Union. Take your time. Remember, no one so far this evening has answered all three questions correctly. So there are the prizes, and here is your big chance. Now, for the prize how many States are comprised by the expression the U.S.A.?'

Peggy considered carefully. She ran the tip of her tongue across her lips, then:

'Forty-eight States,' she said.

The glass box that prevented her receiving tips from the audience also protected her from its composite sound of exasperation. Charles Hassop looked professionally saddened. Having, as well as sound ideas on public relations, quite a natural kindly disposition towards his victims, he stretched a point to ask, tentatively:

'You've told us that there are forty-eight States in the Union. You feel quite sure forty-eight is the number you meant?'

Peggy in her glass box nodded.

'Sure I do – but I don't think it is very fair of you, either,' she told him.

Mr Hassop arrested his incipient expression of compassion to inquire:

'Not fair?'

'No,' said Peggy stoutly. 'For was it not "no trick questions" you were telling us just now? And is it not "fifty" you are after trying to make me say this minute?'

Mr Hassop stared at her for a moment.

'Well,' he began, but she cut him short.

'It was forty-eight States I said, and 'tis forty-eight States I say still,' affirmed Peggy. 'Forty-eight States, and *two* Commonwealths, *and* the District of Columbia,' she added, decisively.

Mr Hassop had a glazed look. He opened his mouth to reply, hesitated, and thought better of it. He knew what the card said, but a possible predicament was suddenly revealed ghastly clear, a pitfall at his feet. With an effort he imitated his usual aplomb.

'Just a minute, please,' he told the audience, and stepped hastily to the side of the platform to confer.

When the performance was over they all went back to the Ballyloughrish Castle Hotel for supper – all, that is, except Mr Hassop who had left them after congratulating Peggy on her winnings in a rather guarded way.

'Miss MacRafferty,' said the nice Irish young man who was again her neighbour, 'I had already observed you to have a disproportionate share of our national charm, now may I congratulate you upon equal felicity with our national luck?'

'I'm sure that is very kind of you, indeed – even though everybody there, except a few of your people, was Irish, too,' Peggy told him. 'Besides, I did know the answer.'

'Sure, you did – and 'tis as clever as pretty you are,' he agreed. 'But, after all, it *might* have been a different question, you know.' He paused, and chuckled. 'Poor dear Charles. The trick question he knows very well, in spite of what he says, but the trick answer is a nasty new experience for him, and he near-as-a-toucher bought it, too. They had to ring up the U.S. Consulate in Dublin, and he's still sweating slightly.'

'Is it trying to tell me it was not a trick question, you are?' demanded Peggy.

He looked at her thoughtfully for a moment, and decided it might be simpler to change the subject.

'What will you be doing with all your loot?' he inquired.

'Well,' she said, 'we don't have the electricity at Barranacleugh, but I am thinking the deep-freezer would make a lovely corn-bin.'

'Without doubt,' he agreed.

'But those paper things are just cheating,' she added.

'You mean the year's free supply of Titania Cobweb Decosmeticizing Tissues? I don't quite see –'

'But, of course. Don't you see, what they are hoping is that I shall spend all the money on cosmi – cosmics – cosmetics so that I can wipe them off free. Well, I shall not. It is what they call in America a racket,' she explained.

'Ah, I'd not thought of that,' he admitted. 'But the money – I hope that's all right?' he added with concern.

Peggy took the cheque from her bag and smoothed it out on the table. He, she, and the young Englishman on her other side, looked at it respectfully.

'Sure,' she said. 'That is very nice. 'Tis me darling fortune. Half a grand, as they say in America.'

'Five hundred nicker is a lot better than half an American grand, and very nice to have,' agreed the Irish young man. 'But scarcely a fortune, you know. Not these days. Still, no tax – and that's where we're one up on America, too. What will you be doing with it?'

'Oh, I'll be taking myself to America and going on the films – movies they call them there,' Peggy explained.

The Irish young man shook his head reproachfully.

'You mean television,' he said. 'Films are passés, corny, vieux jeux, old rope.'

'I *don't* mean television. I've just been on that. I mean the films,' Peggy told him firmly.

'But look here –' he said, and proceeded to argue his case eloquently. Peggy heard him out politely, but when he had finished:

''Tis loyal you are,' she told him, 'but 'tis still the films I am meaning.'

'But do you know anyone there?' he asked.

Peggy started on a list of her uncles and cousins, but he cut it short.

'No, I mean anyone in films, in Hollywood? You see, nice as five hundred pounds is, it won't keep you very long out there.'

Peggy had to admit that as far as she knew, none of her relatives was actually concerned with films.

'Well –' he began, but at this point the English young man who had been regarding her thoughtfully for some time without speaking, broke in to say:

'Are you serious about the films? It's a tough life, you know.'

'Maybe I'll be ready for the soft life when I get a bit older,' Peggy told him.

'And Hollywood's full of would-be stars checking hats,' he added.

'And some who are not,' replied Peggy stoutly.

He sank into thought for a time, but presently reverted to the subject.

'Look here,' he said, 'I don't think you quite know what you'd be up against, and how much it would cost. Now, wouldn't it be better to try to break into English films, and try to go on from there?'

'Is that easier, then?'

'It might be. I happen to know a film director –'

'Now, now,' said the Irish young man. 'That's dated, too.' The other ignored him.

'His name,' he went on, 'is George Floyd –'

'Oh, yes. I've heard of him,' said Peggy with aroused interest. 'He did *Passion for Three* in Italy, didn't he?'

'That's it. I could give you an introduction. Of course, I can't guarantee anything, but from something he was saying the other day I think it *might* be worth your while to see him, if you'd like to.'

'Oh, yes –' said Peggy eagerly.

'Er – look here, old boy –' began the other young man, but the English man turned on him.

'Don't be a clot, Michael. Can't you see the tie-up? If George Floyd takes her on, the Popular Amalgamated Television has uncovered a new film star. Every time she's mentioned, there's "the Pop. Amal. Telly discovery" after her name. That's *worth* something. Anyway, it's worth their while to take a chance on it, and get her over to London, and put her up in a good hotel for a week. Even if George doesn't play they'll get some publicity out of it, and it needn't cost her a penny. But I think it's very likely he will play. From the way he was talking she could be just what he's looking for. And she mugs well, too; I looked at the monitor.'

Both of them turned to study Peggy with severely professional regards. Presently the Irish young man said:

'Do you know? I think you've got something . . .' with a serious conviction which started Peggy blushing until she discovered he was addressing his colleague.

After that, though, they stopped being professional, and it was a lovely evening right up to the time they took her home in a car, to the astonishment of those still awake in Barranacleugh.

A week later there came another, and longer, typewritten letter. After congratulating her on her success, it informed her that a proposition laid before the Board of Popular Amalgamated Television, Ltd, by Mr Robbins, whom she would doubtless recall, had been approved. The Company therefore had great pleasure in inviting her, etc., and hoped that the following arrangements would be acceptable. . . . A car would call for her at Barranacleugh at 8 a.m. on the morning of Wednesday, the 16th. . . .

Enclosed with the letter was an air-ticket from Dublin to London, and, pinned to it, a handwritten note which said: 'Worked like a charm so far. Brush up your Yeats. Will meet you London Airport – Bill Robbins.'

A wave of excitement swept through the village, only slightly modified by the general inability to understand what Peggy's Yeats might be.

'But, never mind,' said Eileen, after consideration. ''Tis likely 'tis the English way of sayin' to get a perm. So I'd try that.'

And on Wednesday, sure enough, a car arrived, and Peggy was swept away in it more elegantly than any previous emigrant had ever left Barranacleugh.

In the London airport arrival-hall there was Mr Robbins, waving a hand in greeting, and making his way through the crowd to greet her.

Somebody let off a quite alarming flash, and then Peggy found herself being introduced to a large, comfortable-looking lady in a black suit and a silver fox fur.

'Mrs Trump,' explained Mr Robbins. 'Mrs Trump's function is to guide you, advise you, look after you generally, and fight off the wolves.'

'Wolves?' said Peggy, startled.

'Wolves,' he assured her, 'the place is crawling with 'em.'

She suddenly understood.

'Oh, I see. You mean the American kind that whistle?' she asked.

'Well, that's how they *start*. Though they come under all flags, I assure you.'

Then she, and Mr Robbins, and Mrs Trump, and an unhappy-looking man with a camera who was just known as Bert, all got into a big car, and were driven off.

'Our people fell for it in quite a big way,' Mr Robbins told Peggy. 'In about a couple of hours' time you meet the Press. Day after tomorrow I've fixed up for you to see George Floyd. But not a word about him to the Press boys and girls. Watch that. It wouldn't do to look as if we were trying to force his hand. And there's a one-minute spot for you on our programme tomorrow night.

'Just now, however, we've got to think up something to tell the Press about you. What about your family, for instance? Have they played any important part in history? Soldiers? Sailors? Explorers?'

Peggy thought.

'Well, there was me great-great-grandfather. He went to Someone's land. Would that be exploring, now?'

'Not in the usual sense. And some time ago, too. Something more recent?'

Peggy reconsidered.

'There was some of me mother's brothers that were grand at burnin' the English houses,' she suggested.

'Not quite the angle, perhaps. Try again,' urged Mr Robbins.

'I don't know – oh, there was my Uncle Sean, of course. He was quite famous.'

'What did he do? Blow things up?' inquired Bert hopefully.

'Oh, I don't think so. But he got himself shot in the end by another very famous man called Al Capone,' Peggy said.

The Consort Hotel, when they reached it, turned out to be a proud place indeed, but they went through the foyer with an accomplished flying-wedge to avoid any journalist who might be trying to jump the gun, and were whizzing upwards before Peggy could really take it in.

'Would this be an elevator, now?' she inquired with interest.

'It could be – though if the Americans had run really true to form it would be a Vertical Personnel Distributor. *We* call it a lift,' Bert told her.

In a thickly carpeted corridor they paused outside a numbered door, and Mrs Trump spoke for the first time.

'Now you two. Beat it into the sitting-room. And keep sober,' she instructed.

'You've got just half an hour, Dulcie. No more,' Mr Robbins told her.

They entered a luxurious room which was mostly shades of grey-green with gold pickings. A girl in a neat black silk dress was already there, and, laid out on the iridescent eiderdown, were a smart grey suit, a green silk dress, and a long, shining white frock.

'We've got to get cracking, Honor,' announced Mrs Trump. 'Turn on that bath. And she'd better wear the green.'

Peggy went to the bed, lifted the green dress, and held it against her.

''Tis a darlin' dress, Mrs Trump, and just right for me. How did you know?'

'Mr Robbins told us your size and colouring. So we chanced it.'

'Well, 'tis very clever you all are to be sure. I expect you must have had lots of experience of looking after girls like me.'

'Well, I was twelve years in the Service,' Mrs Trump told her, as she struggled out of her jacket and cleared for action.

'In the W.R.A.C.?' asked Peggy.

'No, Holloway,' said Mrs Trump. 'Now come along, dearie, we've none too much time.'

'Keep *still*,' instructed Bert, and went on crouching, and creeping about the carpet.

'Modern photographer's ritual dance,' explained Mr Robbins.

'You don't have to turn to face me,' said Bert, from his knees. 'What I'm after is the three-quarter. Hold it like that.' He shuffled round a bit. 'Now take the pose.'

Peggy stood rigidly still. Bert lowered his camera, wearily.

'Be jabers, would they be after not having cameras at all, at all, in Barranacleugh?' he inquired.

'They would not,' Peggy told him.

'All right. We'll start from first principles then. Stand where you are. Put your arms behind your back and clasp your hands together. Now look down here at the camera. That's right. Now press your elbows closer together, and smile. No, better than that: every tooth you've got. Never mind if it feels like a ghastly grin to you, the art editor knows best. That's more like it. Now hold the smile. Keep pressing your elbows together, and take a deep breath, deep as you can. That the best you can do? It looks almost normal – oh well. . . .'

There was a vivid flash. Peggy relaxed.

'Was that all right?'

'You'll be surprised,' said Bert. 'We can teach nature a thing or two, we can.'

'It seems a lot of fadiddle just for a photograph,' said Peggy.

Bert looked at her.

'Mavourneen,' he said, 'have you *seen* a photograph lately?' He reached for a picture-paper and flipped over a page or two. 'Voilà!' he said, handing it across.

'Oh,' said Peggy. 'D'you mean it's like that I'll be looking?'

'That is what I mane – mean, damn it – more or less,' Bert assured her.

Peggy continued to study the picture.

'Would she be kind of gone wrong now – deformed, do they call it?' she inquired.

'This,' Bert told her severely, 'is called glamour – or glamor – and any more heresy or sacrilege out of you, young woman, and you'll find yourself booked for the stake.'

'What they call in America the hot-squat?' Peggy suggested.

Mr Robbins intervened.

'Come,' he said, 'there is another qualification for the hot-squat, and that is to keep the Press waiting. Now remember what we agreed in the car. And keep off the drinks. They're meant to soften them up, not us.'

'Well,' said Mr Robbins, relaxing. 'That's that. Now *we* can have a drink. Mrs Trump? Miss MacRafferty?'

'A small port and lemon, please,' said Mrs Trump.

'Er – a highball, with rye,' said Peggy.

Mr Robbins frowned.

'Miss MacRafferty, your studies appear to have been extensive, but erratic. You mustn't mix your territories. I shall not translate. I shall recommend for you the product of our native Mr Pimm.'

When the drinks arrived he sank half his own triple whisky with satisfaction.

'Pretty good, Bert?' he remarked.

'Good enough,' agreed the photographer, but without enthusiasm. 'Not bad at all. Yes, you did nicely, Mavourneen. You're all set.'

Peggy brightened a little.

'Is that the truth, now? I was thinking most of them – the important ones – were not noticing me at all.'

'Don't you believe it, my dear. They notice. Though it doesn't matter much about the men. It's the sisters you want to watch, particularly if they come at you sweetly – and they didn't.' He emptied his glass, and held it out to be refilled. 'Funny thing about them and girls. There's a kind of girl that'll bring all their claws out at fifty yards; another that'll set them wrinkling their noses at twenty; then there's a bigger lot that doesn't register much – just the new crop coming into the old mill; and every now and then there's one that makes 'em go absent-minded for a moment. "The things that I have seen I now can see no more." Gives you quite a jolt to realize that even for them there was once a glimpse of the celestial light. Sic transit treviter gloria mundi.' He sighed.

'In vino morbida,' observed Mr Robbins.

'You mean tristitia,' suggested Bert.

'And what the devil would the both of you be talking about at all?' inquired Peggy.

'The fleeting moment, my dear,' Bert told her. He groped beside his chair, and swung up his camera. 'But fast as it flits I can make at least its shadow stand. I now propose to take one or two *real* pictures.'

'Oh dear, I thought all that was over,' said Peggy.

'Perhaps soon – but not yet, not quite,' Bert told her, holding up his meter.

Well, even if English people were a little mad, they had been quite kind and nice to her. So Peggy put down her glass, and stood up. She shook out her skirt, patted her hair, and took up the pose as before.

'Like that?' she asked him.

'No,' said Bert. '*Not* like that. . . .'

The next day Peggy had her television 'spot', wearing the white brocade dress – 'our recent prizewinner who will soon be winning prizes on the screen too' – and everyone was very nice and kind about it, and seemed to think it had gone well.

Then the following day there was the interview with Mr Floyd, who turned out to be nice, too, though there was really much more to it than just an interview. She had not expected to have to walk about and sit down and get up and register this and that in front of cameras quite so soon, but Mr Floyd seemed quite pleased and Mr Robbins patted her shoulder as they left, and said: 'Good girl! I sometimes wish *I* could look as if

D

I were seeing fairies in w13, but I suppose I'd be misunderstood.'

In a gesture well known to the industry George Floyd ran his fingers through his profuse, greying hair.

'After those tests, you've got to admit she *has* something,' he insisted. 'She's definitely photogenic, she can move well, she looks fresh. If she doesn't know much about acting yet, well nor do most of 'em, and at least she's not picked up any of the regular tricks and gimmicks. She can take direction, she tried; and furthermore she has charm. She could do a pretty job, and I'd like to use her.'

Solly de Kopf removed his cigar.

'I'll allow she's a good looker in her way,' he admitted, 'but she ain't contemporary like the customers expect. She talks kinda funny, too,' he added.

'A bit of speech-training'll take care of that all right. She's not dumb,' said George.

'Maybe. What do you think of her, Al?' Solly inquired of his henchman.

Al Foster said judicially:

'She mugs well,' he admitted. 'Good height, nice legs. But it's like you said, Chief, she ain't contemporary. But her middle number's okay – around twenty-two, I reckon. That's the important one, the others fix pretty easy. I'll say she *could* do, Chief. Ain't no Lolo, though.'

'Hell, why *should* she be a Lolo?' George inquired. 'Imitation Lolos are practically a major Italian export. It's getting time somebody put up something different, and she could be it.'

'Different?' said Solly, suspiciously.

'Different,' repeated George, firmly. 'There's a time when these things work themselves out. You should know, Solly – remember what happened to *Spotlight on My Heart*? That was a sure-fire, night-club-star epic – only it happened to be your ninth, and it didn't fire. It's time we gave Italian romance a rest for a bit.'

'But Italy ain't worked out yet. It's still big money,' de Kopf objected. 'Why, right now Al's on to a thing called *The Stones of Venice* we're aiming to buy just as soon as we can locate a copy and sign up the author. And before that we've got a regular blown in the bottle sex number lined up. Seems the Romans – the old Romans, not this present lot – were short on women some way, so they cooked up the idea of inviting all the guys from the next city over to some kind of stag-party, and then while the fun was on they sent out a gang that rounded up all the other guys' wives, and made off with 'em. Lot of scope there; real genuine historical incident, too. I had that checked, so it's classical and okay. We'll have to find a new title, though. It's shocking what they let 'em get away with in books – just imagine trying to get past with a *picture* called *The Rape of the Sabrinas*.

'Well,' conceded George, 'if you can get it done in time, maybe the sight of a couple of hundred Lolos dashing about in a shrieking panic and the near-nude will give the teen-agers a kick –'

'Not maybe, George. It's got history, like *The Ten Commandments*; and all the rest, too. It's sure-fire.'

'You could be right this time, Solly – but if you quarry away at Italy much longer you're going to have another *Spotlight*. It's getting to time for a fresh angle.'

Solly de Kopf pondered heavily.

'What you say to that, Al?'

'Could be, Chief. It gets like it looks they'll take a line for ever until one day – whammo, it's out,' Al admitted.

'And we're in the cart again,' added George. 'Look, Solly, once upon a time we had 'em all, all sizes and ages of 'em, going to the movies twice a week, year in, year out. And now look at the industry.'

'Yeh. Goddamned television,' said Solly de Kopf, with weary venom.

'And what did we do about television? Hell, it's not all *that* good. But did we try to save that audience, and keep it in the movie-houses?'

99

'We certainly did. Didn't we give 'em wide screens and super-vision?'

'What we gave 'em was a few gimmicks, and catch-crop corn, Solly. We concentrated on the green teenagers and the arresteds – and that's about all the audience we've got left, except for a few big pictures. We just let the whole of the huge middle-aged audience go, and didn't do a thing to save it.'

'So what? You're exaggerating, as usual, George, but you've got a bit of something.'

'So this, Solly. There are still middle-aged people in the world, more in fact, than there were, and nobody's catering for 'em. Everybody's on the same racket, fighting to fleece the kids: us, the record people, the tin-pan alley boys, the mike-moaners, the espresso-bars, the jazz dives, the picture-papers, and I'd not exclude the Proms: even the telly shovels over a high percentage of adolescent drip. And here's this whole later age-group with practically nothing being done about it – and this is the age-group that brought the industry millions by sighing and having a nice weep over *Smilin' Through*, *Rose of Tralee*, *Lilly of Killarney*, *Daddy Long Legs*, *Comin' Through the Rye*, and the like. That's what's wanted, Solly. The lump in the throat, a wistful tear, the gentle hand on the heart-strings. Give 'em the right stuff, and they'll love it. We'll have 'em back in the movie-houses, sobbing in the aisles. And I think this girl could do it.'

'Re-makes, huh?' said Solly, thoughtfully.

'No,' said George, '*not* just re-makes. That's the mistake other guys have paid for. It's the same age-group we're after, with the same emotion-factor, but it's a different generation – so the triggers aren't the same – not quite. We've got to figure out what the modern triggers are – or we'll just get corn.'

'Huh,' said Solly de Kopf again, and non-committally. 'What do you think, Al?'

'Could be something in it, Chief,' admitted Al. He looked at George, keenly. 'You're saying to make romance romantic instead of sexy? Well, that's quite an angle.'

'Of course it's an angle. The woman who weeps at weddings is a folk-figure. As I said, we'll not promote a good modern heartache by doing it just the way they went about it in the twenties, but I'm damned sure that if we tackle it right a revival of Celtic nostalgia could go across big.'

'H'm. You'll not set any box-offices on fire with a name like Margaret MacRafferty, will he, Al?' Solly remarked.

'That's so, Chief,' Al pondered. 'What about Connie O'Mara?' he suggested.

'No,' said George decidedly, 'that's just the thing to avoid. It's a period name, like Peggy O'Neil, or Gracie Fields, or Kitty O'Shea – too homey. It's got to have glamour, and a fey touch, too, but you needn't worry. I've fixed that.'

'How?' Al inquired.

'Deirdre Shilsean,' announced George.

'Come again?' said Mr de Kopf.

George wrote it down in large capitals, and pushed it across. Solly de Kopf studied it.

'I don't see how that makes "Shilshawn," do you?' he inquired of Al who was peering over his shoulder.

'The Irish do that sort of thing,' George explained.

'It's got class,' Al admitted, 'but you can't get away with it. Not a hope. Look what they did with Diane, and that's simple – or Marie, for that matter. One decko at this, and she'll be Dye-dree Shilseen.'

Solly de Kopf, however, continued to regard the name.

'I like it,' he said. 'It *looks* good.'

'But, Chief –'

'I know, Al. Ease off. If the customers like to call Diane, Dye-ann, and this one Dye-dree, what the hell! They pay to call 'em what they like, don't they? But it still *looks* good.'

'Well, you're the chief, Chief. But there's more to it than a name,' Al told him.

'She's willing to go to Marinstein,' said George.

'Huh. Aren't they all?' said Mr de Kopf.

'And she's ready to pay for the course,' added George.

'That's better,' admitted Solly.

'But she can't run to living expenses as well.'

'Pity,' said Solly de Kopf.

'However, Pop. Amal. Telly would be willing to advance her that, as an investment,' said George.

Solly de Kopf's eyebrows lowered, and approached one another.

'What the hell business is it of theirs?' he demanded.

'Well, they discovered her, on one of their quiz things,' George explained.

Solly went on frowning.

'So now they're out to grab our stars even before they are stars, are they?' he growled. 'The hell they are! Al, see this girl gets a contract – an option contract, contingent on her getting a Marinstein certificate, and us being satisfied – don't commit us. We stake her for living exes – and see it's a *good* hotel – not one of the lousy ones that telly lot'd choose. Fix it so she does it with class, and tell the publicity boys they got to get working on her fast. And don't forget to let Marinstein know we'll be looking for a ten-per-cent rebate. Got that?'

'Sure, Chief. Right away,' said Al, making for the door.

Solly de Kopf turned back to George.

'Well, there's your star,' he said. 'Now what's the story you've got for her?'

'It'll have to be written yet,' George acknowledged. 'But that'll be easy. It's her I want. She'll be a pretty colleen with the simplicity of a child, heart of gold, etcetera; in a background of the emerald fields and the purple mists on the mountains and the blue smoke rising from the cabins. She's vulnerable and unsophisticated, and she sings plaintive airs as she milks the cow, but she has a touch of innate ancestral wisdom over the ways of life and death, and a disposition to love lambs and believe in leprechauns. She could have a brother, a wild boy, who gets into trouble running bombs over the border, and she goes, pale, innocent, and heartrending, to plead for him. And when she meets this officer –'

'What officer?' inquired Solly de Kopf.

'The officer who arrested him, of course. When she meets him, a kind of primeval spark ignites between them. . . .'

'There it is,' said the girl beside Peggy. 'That's Marinstein.'

Peggy looked out. Under the tilt of the aircraft's wing lay a town of white houses with pink roofs clustered on the bank of a wide, winding river. Somewhat back from the river rose an abrupt mass of rock, and, perched upon the rock, a building with towers and turrets and crenellations and banners floating in the breeze – the Castle of Marinstein guarding, as it had guarded these twelve hundred years and more, its town, and the ten square miles of the principality.

'Isn't it *thrilling*! Marinstein!' said the girl, in a gush of breath.

The aircraft touched-down, ran along the concrete, and taxied to a stop in front of the airport building. There was a great deal of chattering and collecting of belongings, then the passengers descended. At the foot of the steps Peggy stopped to look round.

It was a magic scene, lit by bright, warm sunshine. In the background rose the dark bulk of the rock and its castle, dominating everything. In the foreground, gleaming coral white, almost to hurt the eyes, stood the airport building, its central tower surmounted by a huge, but somewhat slendered, version of the Venus of Milo. In front of it, on a tall flagstaff wafted the Ducal Standard, and across the dazzling façade of the building itself ran the inscription:

BIENVENU A MARINSTEIN – CITÉ DE BEAUTÉ
(Marinstein the Beauty City Welcomes You)

The baggage-hall was a concatenation of her travelling companions. The only men in sight were a few white-coated porters. One of these noticed the bright labels upon Peggy's bags, pounced upon them, and led her to the exit.

'La voiture de Ma'mselle Shilsène,' he bawled impressively.

Half the place stopped its chattering to look at Peggy, with awe, or envy, or thoughtful calculation. Publicity had been busy over Plantagenet Films' new find, with a wide circulation of photographs. There had been reports of Peggy's contract that looked considerably firmer in newsprint than they did on the form of Agreement. So already the name Deirdre Shilsean was not unknown to those who keep a close eye on these things.

A magnificent car swept to the kerb. The porter handed Peggy into it, and presently she was whirled up to the Grand Hotel Narcisse which perched on a shoulder of the rock, just below the castle itself. There, she was ushered to an exquisite room, with a beflowered balcony that looked out over the town, and across the river and the plain beyond. There was a petal-pink bathroom, too, with big bottles of coloured salts, flasks of essences, bowls of powder, gleaming fittings, and enormous warmed towels, that surpassed anything Peggy had ever dreamed of. A maid turned on the water. Peggy shed her clothes, and stretched out with luxurious bliss in the bath that was like the nacred pink interior of a shell.

The sound of a gong caused her eventually to leave it. Back in the bedroom she put on the long white dress that she had worn for the television spot, and went down to dinner.

It was rather odd being in a sumptuous dining-room where the only men were the waiters, and all the ladies spent their time studying one another more or less covertly, and a bit boring, too. So when the waiter suggested she should have her coffee on the terrace she took his advice.

The sun had set an hour since. A half-moon was up, and the river caught its gleam. On an island in the river stood a delicate little open temple where concealed lighting illuminated a snowy figure standing meditatively, with an apple in her hand. Peggy assumed it to be Eve, but though the sculptor had had Atalanta in mind, the error was not significant.

The town itself was a-spangle with little lights; and small neon signs, too far off to be read, blinked intermittently. Further away the floodlit Venus on the airport tower hovered like a ghost. Behind was the black bulk of the rock, with the turret lights of the castle seeming to hang in the sky. Peggy sighed.

''Tis all like magic – so it is,' she said.

A solitary, somewhat older, woman at the next table glanced at her.

'You're new here?' she inquired.

Peggy admitted that she had just arrived.

'I wish I had – or, maybe, I wish I never had,' said the lady. 'This is my seventh time, and more than enough.'

'I think it's lovely,' said Peggy, 'but if you don't like it, why would you be coming here, at all?'

'Because my friends come here – for the annual refit. Maybe you'll have heard of the Joneses?'

'I don't know any Joneses,' said Peggy. 'Would they be your friends?'

'They're the people I have to live with,' said the woman. She looked at Peggy again. 'You're still very young, my dear, so they'd likely not interest you a lot right now, but you'll be meeting them socially later on.'

Peggy perceived no reply to that, so she passed it.

'You're American, are you not?' she asked. 'That must be wonderful. I've a lot of relatives there I've never seen. But I hope I'll be going there myself before too long, now.'

'You can have it,' the lady told her. 'Me, I'll take Paris, France.'

Abruptly the light changed, and, looking up, Peggy saw that the castle was now floodlit with a peach-coloured glow.

'Oh, 'tis beautiful – like a fairy palace, it is,' she exclaimed.

'Sure,' said the lady, without enthusiasm. 'That's the idea.'

'But romantic, it all is,' said Peggy. 'The moon – and the river – and the lights – and the wonderful smell of all the flowers. . . .'

'Friday night it's Chany's "Number Seven",' said the lady. 'Tomorrow it'll be Revigant's "Fury" – a little vulgar that, I think, but then everything everywhere is downgraded a bit on Saturday nights, isn't it? Co-adjustment to the increased consumer-potential of the lower-income-brackets, I guess.

105

Sundays are better – Cotinson's "Devotée", kind of cleaner. They puff it out from the castle turrets,' she explained, 'except when the wind's the other way; then they puff it from the airport tower.'

'This great profession of ours,' Madame Letitia Chaline once memorably said, at a lunch-time address to the International Association of Practising Beauticians, 'this calling of ours is a very great deal more than an industry. Indeed, one might call it a spiritual force that gives women faith. Tearfully, tearfully, from beyond the dawn of history unhappy women have sent up their prayers for beauty, all too seldom answered – but now, and to us, has been granted the power to give these prayers results, to bring comfort to unhappy millions of our sisters. This, my friends, is a solemn reflection. . . .'

And as evidence of the faith created there were the bottles and pots, sachets and tubes of Letitia Chaline Beauty Ancillaries gracing shop windows, dressing-tables, and handbags from Seattle to Helsinki to Lisbon to Tokio, and even subtly discoverable, though at a price and in shades several years behind the rest of the world's fashion, at such places as Omsk. Elegant Chaline shrines, stationed with a good sense of real estate value, gleamed seductively in New York, London, Rio, Paris, Rome, and a dozen more leading cities, the administrative centres of an empire which had hated rivals in co-existence, but no more worlds to conquer.

In the offices and salons of these buildings the work of calling beauty into existence went on in a state of nervous torque, for it was always possible that on any day Letitia Chaline herself (or Lettice Scheukelman, as her passport described her) might drop from the sky with scourges, and a cohort of efficiency experts. And yet, in spite of system and pressure, it seemed that the limit of expansion other than the little fillips gained by gobbling up an occasional small rival, had been reached – at least, so it had seemed until Letitia's daughter, Miss Cathy Scheukelman (or Chaline) married an impoverished European, and so became Her Highness the Grand Duchess Katerina of Marinstein.

Cathy had not actually seen Marinstein before she married it, and when she did, it came as something of a shock. The castle had a fine romantic manner, but was about as comfortable to inhabit as a suite of caves. The town was badly run down, and its inhabitants occupied almost entirely with begging, sleeping, procreation, and vines; in the rest of the realm it was much the same, except that there was no one to beg from.

Many a Grand Duchess in similar circumstances has squeamed, and taken-off for an established centre of gracious living; Cathy, however, came of enterprising stock. At her world-famous mother's knee she had absorbed not only the gospel of Beauty, but a useful working knowledge of the principles of big business, as was suitable for one who would later have considerable holdings in Letitia Chaline and its ramifications. And as she sat in her castle turret, looking out over penurious Marinstein, there sounded within her an echo of that enterprising idealism which had inspired her mother to confer the blessing of beauty upon womankind. After an hour's cogitation she reached a verdict.

'Momma,' she said, addressing that absent though world-wide spirit, 'Momma, dear, you're no green pasture, but I guess you don't have this thing sewn right up. Not even yet.'

And she sent for her secretary, and started to dictate letters.

Three months later the airfield had been graded, and the concrete apron was being spread, the Grand Duchess had laid the stone of the first hotel, strange machines were cutting drainage trenches in the streets, and the Marinsteiners were attending a series of compulsory lectures on hygiene and civic responsibility.

Five years later there were, in addition to two first-class hotels, and two second-class hotels, three more being built, for it had occurred to the Grand Duchess that as well as social beauty she could supply various kinds of professional beauty along with instruction on its concomitants, and most advantageous deployment. There were half a dozen salles, cliniques, and écoles, permanent or temporary, and the Marinsteiners after severe tutelage were beginning to appreciate the economic theory behind conserving the sources of one's golden eggs.

After ten years there was a clean, but still picturesque, town, a University of Beauty, a world-wide reputation, an expensive clientèle, an acknowledged standard of education in the arts of pulchritude, and a regular air service by the big lines. All over the capitalist world the head of Botticelli's Venus looked from cards in the best coiffeurs', from posters in select travel agencies, from the glossier magazines, urging all who set store by beauty to seek and find it at its very fount, Marinstein. By which time the early prophets of disaster had long turned their minds to promoting the use of their products at Marinstein, with generous acknowledgement that its Grand Duchess was indeed a hair of the old mink.

Thus it was that when Peggy MacRafferty, after a breakfast that had the charm of novelty, but scarcely the amplitude of Irish standards, stepped out of the Grand Hotel Narcisse on her first morning, she saw a scoured cobbled street, white houses with fresh-painted shutters, flowers tumbling over their walls, bright-striped awnings on the shops, with the sun over all. She was impelled to wave aside the waiting taxis. Another girl emerging at the same time did likewise, and glancing at Peggy, exclaimed:

'Oh, isn't it a lovely, lovely place! I'd much rather walk, and see it all.'

Which was a pleasant change from the blasé lady of the previous evening, so that Peggy warmed to her, and they set off down the town together.

On the south side of the Place d'Artemis (formerly the Hochgeborenprinzadelbertplatz) stood a gracefully pillared building with a facia that announced: ENREGISTREMENTS.

'I suppose that's it,' said Peggy's companion. 'It does feel a bit like going in for an exam, doesn't it?'

At a large counter in the hall a tall soignée lady received them with a somewhat intimidating manner.

'Social,' she inquired, 'stage, screen, model, professional television, or freelance?'

'Screen,' said Peggy and the other girl, simultaneously.

The soignée lady signed to a small page.

'Take these ladies to Miss Cardew,' she told him.

'I'm glad you're screen, too,' said the girl. 'My name's Pat – I mean, Carla Carlita.'

'Mine's – er – Deirdre Shilsean,' Peggy told her.

The girl's eyes widened.

'Oh, that's wonderful. I've read about you. You've got a real contract with Plantagenet Films, haven't you? The others were talking about it on the plane, only I didn't realize it was you. They're all green with envy. I am, too. Oh, I think it's thrilling –' She was cut short by the child ushering them into a room, and announcing: 'Two ladies to see you, Miss Cardew.'

At first glance the room contained little but a couple of chairs, a luxurious carpet, and a floral riot on a large desk. Round this, however, a face presently peered to say: 'Please sit down.'

Peggy did so, in a position from which she was able to see the unencumbered end of the desk, and also the neat card that announced: 'Flower Tone-Poems by Persistence Fry, Rue de la Pompadour 10 (Individual Tuition).' They gave their names, and Miss Cardew consulted a book.

'Ah, yes,' she said, 'we have you both programmed. Now, your courses will consist partly of private treatments, and partly of classes. For details of these you should see Miss Arbuthnot at the Callisthenium. . . .'

There was quite a list of instructors and directors, ending up with Miss Higgins for elocution.

'Miss Higgins,' exclaimed Peggy, 'is she Irish?'

'I really could not say,' admitted Miss Cardew, 'but she is, as are all our staff, of course, an expert in her field – a grand-daughter of the famous Professor Henry Higgins. Now I'll ring

Miss Arbuthnot and try to fix you an appointment for this afternoon.'

Peggy and Carla bought some stamps with a very pretty engraving of Botticelli's Venus's head on them, although printed in mauve, and then spent an hour inspecting a variety of boutiques, salons, maisons, ateliers, coins, and even étals, before adjourning to the riverside restaurant, Aux Milles Bateaux, at the foot of the Boulevarde de la Belle Hélène, to put in the rest of their time until their appointment. Mostly, they talked films, with Carla showing a flattering interest in every detail that Peggy could recall of her contract.

Miss Arbuthnot at the Callisthenium turned out to be a rather severe featured lady who regarded one with dispassion and an eye under which it was hard not to feel misshapen.

'H'm,' she said, after consideration.

Peggy began nervously:

'Och, I know my vital statistics aren't quite –' but Miss Arbuthnot cut her short.

'I'm afraid that is not a term we favour,' she said. 'In Marinstein we prefer to speak of one's Indices of Beauty. Your waist I judge as satisfactory at 22, but it will need your serious attention to enable you to attain 42–22–38.'

'Forty-two!' exclaimed Peggy. 'Oh, I don't think –'

'It is not a question of personal taste,' said Miss Arbuthnot. 'As the Grand Duchess has often remarked of our social side: to be seen wearing last year's shape is worse than driving last year's model. On the screen side one must be even more requirement-conscious. For contemporary screen requirements 42–22–38 *is* beauty; anything else is *not*.'

'But forty-two –' Peggy protested.

'Oh, we shall achieve it for you. After all, that is why we are here, isn't it?'

Peggy supposed, a little uncertainly, that it must be.

'Now,' said Miss Arbuthnot after she had given her the callisthenics timetable, 'I expect you'll want to see Miss Carnegie, your personality-coach.'

On leaving, Peggy found the ante-room outside thronged

with waiting girls. She heard her new name mentioned by several of them as she passed through. It should have been flattering, but somehow it was not; they were all watching her very carefully.

'Light vivacity, light vivacity, just say it to yourself over and over again whenever you're doing nothing in particular – and even if you are.'

'But is that *really* my personality? Is it the real *me*?' asked Peggy.

Miss Carnegie raised her eyebrows.

'*Your* personality?' she said, then she smiled. 'Oh, I see. Oh dear, you have got a lot to learn, haven't you? You're confusing us with the television side, I'm afraid. Screen personality is *quite* different. Oh, yes, indeed. A few years ago it was sultry, then we had sparkling for a time, then we had a stretch of sincerity – let me see what came next? Oh, yes, smouldering, and, for a rather brief time, ingenuousness – but that doesn't suit modern audiences, silly to try it, really – then there was a spell of passionpent – the audiences liked that all right, but it was exceedingly trying for everyone else. This season it's lightly-vivacious. So just keep on saying it to yourself until you come to me again next Wednesday. Light-vivacity, light-vivacity! Try to throw your weight a little more forward on your toes, you'll find that'll help. Light-vivacity, light-vivacity!'

And then to her coiffeur, to her facial-artist, to her deportment-instructor, to her dietician, to a number of others until, finally, to Miss Higgins, whom she found on the point of terminating an interview with Carla.

'Yes,' Miss Higgins was saying. 'You've a good ear. I don't think you will need much help from me. We can easily emphasize those "Rs" a little. What you need to guard against is a tendency to shout in ordinary conversation. That's hard on the microphone. Besides, unless she happens to live in Kensington, a lady doesn't shout.'

Then Carla departed, and it was Peggy's turn. Miss Higgins

asked her to read a passage printed on a card, and listened, fascinated.

'Beautiful!' she said. 'I must get you to make some recordings before we spoil it. Those "ees"! Please repeat after me: "The B.B.C. decrees at least three paeans to Greensleeves each week".'

For the next ten minutes Peggy demonstrated her vowels. As she concluded, Miss Higgins was regarding her with the benevolence of one who has at last discovered a task worthy of her talents.

'A work after my grandfather's heart,' she said, 'but it's going to mean hard work for you, my dear. Harder than for any of the rest, I'm afraid.'

'The rest?' asked Peggy.

'Well, there are thirty-six of you on the next Screen Beauty Course, and it is a highly competitive profession, you know.'

'But I do have a contract, Miss Higgins.'

'An *option* contract, I understand,' amended Miss Higgins. 'That makes an extra incentive. I don't suppose you are acquainted with your competitors yet, but they have read all about you, and what is the result? Four of them have already requested that they may be given a slight trace of Irish in their speech, and I have no doubt more will do the same. So you see. . . !'

Peggy stared at her indignantly.

'Have they indeed! So it is after stealing my contract they are?'

'It shows the way the wind blows,' admitted Miss Higgins. 'But, of course,' she added consolingly, 'it is an utterly impossible request. Naturally, one cannot teach anything on this course other than received Anglo-American. Still, it does go to show . . . .'

'But if they change me shape, and change me voice, and change me hair, and change me face, as they say, what is it that is me, at all?' asked Peggy.

'One has a duty to the public,' said Miss Higgins, 'or, perhaps one should say, the film people have a duty to the public. One has to learn to suit oneself to a medium, to work within its limits. That is required of every artist, is it not?'

Peggy unhappily supposed it was.

'Now, don't you worry, my dear,' Miss Higgins advised. 'We'll see you through, and get you your certificate. Just you come along here on Monday morning after your callisthenics, and we'll get down to it. You'll be in movies, all right, never doubt it. . . .'

George Floyd wandered into Mr Solly de Kopf's spacious office, and dropped into an easy-chair.

'What's the matter with you?' Solly inquired looking up.

'I need a drink,' George told him, 'a large one.'

Al conjured it up, and put it beside him.

'What's wrong? I thought you'd gone to meet her. Don't say the Marinstein plane's crashed.'

'Oh, no, it came in all right. Everything was laid on – Press, steam-radio, television, the lot.'

'But she wasn't there?'

'Oh, she was – at least, I think she was.'

Solly de Kopf looked at him with concern.

'George, you gotta get a grip on yourself. You went there to meet her, see that she got properly mugged and all that, and bring her here. Well, where is she?'

George sighed.

'I don't know, Solly. I reckon she's vanished.'

'Al,' said Solly, 'ask him what *happened*.'

'Sure, Chief. Look, George, you say the plane came in all right – then what?'

'It was what came out of it that was the trouble.'

'Well, what did come out of it?'

'Lolos,' said George gloomily. 'Thirty-six made-to-measure Lolos. Not a trace of a colleen, or an Irish Rose among 'em. Thirty-six Lolos, *all* certified up to Marinstein movie-standard, *all* claiming to be Deirdre Shilsean, *all* saying they've got a contract with us. It's heartbreaking.'

'You mean, you can't tell which she is?' inquired Al.

'Well, *you* try – they're all downstairs in the lobby. Anyway, it's too late now if you did. Oh, the blue mountains, the emerald turf, the silver loughs – and the sweet soft-eyed colleen with the laughin' eyes . . . All gone. – Vanished away. Nothing but Lolos.' He sagged further into his chair, radiating a despondency that touched even Solly de Kopf.

Al, however, preserved a thoughtful detachment, and presently he brightened.

'Say, Chief!'

'Huh?' said Solly.

'I been thinking, Chief, maybe that Irish stuff wouldn't have been so hot after all – kinda chancy and out of line. But we do still have a sure-fire script on hand – remember that one about the Roman wolf-pack and the Sabrinas?'

Mr Solly de Kopf sat silent for a moment, teeth clenched on his cigar, then he exhaled, and a gleam came into his eye.

'And thirty-six Lolos waiting in the lobby! Al, you got it! What are we waiting for? Get down there, Al. Get 'em signed up right away – option, mind you, no figures yet.'

'Sure, Chief,' Al said, as he made for the door.

And that is why they keen in the cottage in Barranacleugh by the Slieve Gamph for poor Peggy MacRafferty; her that was lissom as the reeds by the bog, with the sweet trustin' ways of her – her that never was seen again, at all. Ochone!

Stitch in Time

On the sheltered side of the house the sun was hot. Just inside the open french windows Mrs Dolderson moved her chair a few inches, so that her head would remain in the shade while the warmth could comfort the rest of her. Then she leant her head back on the cushion, looking out.

The scene was, for her, timeless.

Across the smooth lawn the cedar stood as it had always stood. Its flat spread boughs must, she supposed, reach a little further now than they had when she was a child, but it was hard to tell; the tree had seemed huge then, it seemed huge now. Farther on, the boundary hedge was just as trim and neat as it had always been. The gate into the spinney was still flanked by the two unidentifiable topiary birds, Cocky and Olly – wonderful that they should still be there, even though Olly's tail feathers had become a bit twiggy with age.

The flower-bed on the left, in front of the shrubbery, was as full of colour as ever – well, perhaps a little brighter; one had a feeling that flowers had become a trifle more strident than they used to be, but delightful nevertheless. The spinney beyond the hedge, however, had changed a little; more young trees, some of the larger ones gone. Between the branches were glimpses of pink roof where there had been no neighbours in the old days. Except for that, one could almost, for a moment, forget a whole lifetime.

The afternoon drowsing while the birds rested, the bees humming, the leaves gently stirring, the bonk-bonk from the tennis court round the corner, with an occasional voice giving the score. It might have been any sunny afternoon out of fifty or sixty summers.

Mrs Dolderson smiled upon it, and loved it all; she had loved it when she was a girl, she loved it even more now.

In this house she had been born; she had grown up in it, married from it, come back to it after her father died, brought up her own two children in it, grown old in it. . . . Some years after the second war she had come very near to losing it – but not quite; and here she still was. . . .

It was Harold who had made it possible. A clever boy, and a wonderful son. . . . When it had become quite clear that she could no longer afford to keep the house up, that it would have to be sold, it was Harold who had persuaded his firm to buy it. Their interest, he had told her, lay not in the house, but in the site – as would any buyer's. The house itself was almost without value now, but the position was convenient. As a condition of sale, four rooms on the south side had been converted into a flat which was to be hers for life. The rest of the house had become a hostel housing some twenty young people who worked in the laboratories and offices which now stood on the north side, on the site of the stables and part of the paddock. One day, she knew, the old house would come down, she had seen the plans, but for the present, for her time, both it and the garden to the south and west could remain unspoilt. Harold had assured her that they would not be required for fifteen or twenty years yet – much longer than she would know the need of them. . . .

Nor, Mrs Dolderson thought calmly, would she be really sorry to go. One became useless, and, now that she must have a wheelchair, a burden to others. There was the feeling, too, that she no longer belonged – that she had become a stranger in another people's world. It had all altered so much; first changing into a place that it was difficult to understand, then growing so much more complex that one gave up trying to understand. No wonder, she thought, that the old become possessive about *things*; cling to objects which link them with the world that they could understand. . . .

Harold was a dear boy, and for his sake she did her best not to appear too stupid – but, often, it was difficult. . . .

Today, at lunch, for instance, he had been so excited about some experiment that was to take place this afternoon. He had *had* to talk about it, even though he must know that practically nothing of what he said was comprehensible to her. Something about dimensions again – she had grasped that much, but she had only nodded, and not attempted to go further. Last time the subject had cropped up, she had observed that in her youth there had been only three, and she did not see how even all this progress in the world could have added more. This had set him off on a dissertation about the mathematician's view of the world through which it was, apparently, possible to perceive the existence of a series of dimensions. Even the moment of existence in relation to time was, it seemed, some kind of dimension. Philosophically, Harold had begun to explain – but there, and at once, she had lost him. He led straight into confusion. She felt sure that when she was young philosophy, mathematics, and metaphysics had all been quite separate studies – nowadays they seemed to have quite incomprehensibly run together. So this time she had listened quietly, making small, encouraging sounds now and then, until at the end he had smiled ruefully, and told her she was a dear to be so patient with him. Then he had come round the table and kissed her cheek gently as he put his hand over hers, and she had wished him the best of luck with the afternoon's mysterious experiment. Then Jenny had come in to clear the table, and wheel her closer to the window. . . .

The warmth of the slumbrous afternoon carried her into a half-dream, took her back fifty years to just such an afternoon when she had sat here in this very window – though certainly with no thought of a wheelchair in those days – waiting for Arthur . . . waiting with an ache in her heart for Arthur . . . and Arthur had never come. . . .

Strange, it was, the way things fell out. If Arthur had come that day she would almost certainly have married him. And then Harold and Cynthia would never have existed. She would have had children, of course, but they would not have been Harold and Cynthia. . . . What a curious, haphazard thing one's existence was. . . . Just by saying 'no' to one man, and 'yes' to another, a woman might bring into existence a potential murderer. . . . How foolish they all were nowadays – trying to tidy everything up, make life secure, while behind, back in everyone's past, stretched the chance-studded line of women who had said 'yes' or 'no', as the fancy took them. . . .

Curious that she should remember Arthur now. It must be years since she had thought of him. . . .

She had been quite sure that he would propose that afternoon. It was before she had even heard of Colin Dolderson. And she would have agreed. Oh yes, she would have accepted him.

There had never been any explanation. She had never known *why* he did not come then – or any more. He had never written to her. Ten days, perhaps a fortnight later there had been a somewhat impersonal note from his mother telling her that he had been ill, and the doctor had advised sending him abroad. But after that, nothing at all – until the day she had seen his name in a newspaper, more than two years later. . . .

She had been angry of course – a girl owed that to her pride – and hurt, too, for a time. . . . Yet how could one know that it had not been for the best, in the end? – Would his children have been as dear to her, or as kind, and as clever as Harold and Cynthia . . . ?

Such an infinity of chances . . . all those genes and things they talked about nowadays. . . .

The thump of tennis-balls had ceased, and the players had gone; back, presumably, to their recondite work. Bees continued to hum purposefully among the flowers; half a dozen butterflies were visiting there too, though in a dilettante, unairworthy-looking way. The farther trees shimmered in the rising heat. The afternoon's drowsiness became irresistible. Mrs Dolderson did not oppose it. She leant her head back, half aware that somewhere another humming sound, higher in pitch than the bees', had started, but it was not loud enough to be disturbing. She let her eyelids drop. . . .

Suddenly, only a few yards away, but out of sight as she sat, there were feet on the path. The sound of them began quite abruptly, as if someone had just stepped from the grass on to the path – only she would have seen anyone crossing the grass. . . . Simultaneously there was the sound of a baritone voice, singing cheerfully, but not loudly to itself. It, too, began quite suddenly; in the middle of a word in fact:

' " – rybody's doin' it, doin' it, do – " '

The voice cut off suddenly. The footsteps, too, came to a dead stop.

Mrs Dolderson's eyes were open now – very wide open. Her thin hands gripped the arms of her chair. She recollected the tune: more than that, she was even certain of the voice – after all these years. . . . A silly dream, she told herself. . . . She had been remembering him only a few moments before she closed her eyes. . . . How foolish . . . !

And yet it was curiously undreamlike. . . . Everything was so sharp and clear, so familiarly reasonable. . . . The arms of the chair quite solid under her fingers. . . .

Another idea leapt into her mind. She had died. That was why it was not like an ordinary dream. Sitting here in the sun, she must have quietly died. The doctor had said it might happen quite unexpectedly. . . . And now it had! She had a swift moment of relief – not that she had felt any great fear of death, but there had been that sense of ordeal ahead. Now it was over – and with no ordeal. As simple as falling asleep. She felt suddenly happy about it; quite exhilarated. . . . Though it was odd that she still seemed to be tied to her chair. . . .

The gravel crunched under shifting feet. A bewildered voice said:

'That's rum! Dashed queer! What the devil's happened?'

Mrs Dolderson sat motionless in her chair. There was no doubt whatever about the voice.

A pause. The feet shifted, as if uncertain. Then they came on, but slowly now, hesitantly. They brought a young man into her view. – Oh, such a very young man, he looked. She felt a little catch at her heart. . . .

He was dressed in a striped club-blazer, and white flannel trousers. There was a silk scarf round his neck, and, tilted back off his forehead, a straw hat with a coloured band. His hands were in his trousers pockets, and he carried a tennis-racket under his left arm.

She saw him first in profile, and not quite at his best, for his expression was bewildered, and his mouth slightly open as he stared towards the spinney at one of the pink roofs beyond.

'Arthur,' Mrs Dolderson said gently.

He was startled. The racket slipped, and clattered on the path. He attempted to pick it up, take off his hat, and recover his composure all at the same time; not very successfully. When he straightened his face was pink, and its expression still confused.

He looked at the old lady in the chair, her knees hidden by a rug, her thin, delicate hands gripping the arms. His gaze went beyond her, into the room. His confusion increased, with a touch of alarm added. His eyes went back to the old lady. She was regarding him intently. He could not recall ever having seen her before, did not know who she could be – yet in her eyes there seemed to be something faintly, faintly not unfamiliar.

She dropped her gaze to her right hand. She studied it for a moment as though it puzzled her a little, then she raised her eyes again to his.

'You don't know me, Arthur?' she asked quietly.

There was a note of sadness in her voice that he took for disappointment, tinged with reproof. He did his best to pull himself together.

'I – I'm afraid not,' he confessed. 'You see I – er – you – er –' he stuck, and then went on desperately: 'You must be Thelma's – Miss Kilder's – aunt?'

She looked at him steadily for some moments. He did not understand her expression, but then she told him:

'No. I am not Thelma's aunt.'

Again his gaze went into the room behind her. This time he shook his head in bewilderment.

'It's all different – no, sort of half-different,' he said, in distress. 'I say, I can't have come to the wrong –?' He broke off, and turned to look at the garden again. 'No, it certainly isn't that,' he answered himself decisively. 'But what – what *has* happened?'

His amazement was no longer simple; he was looking badly shaken. His bewildered eyes came back to her again.

'Please – I don't understand – *how* did you know me?' he asked.

His increasing distress troubled her, and made her careful.

'I recognized you, Arthur. We have met before, you know.'

'Have we? I can't remember. . . . I'm terribly sorry. . . .'

'You're looking unwell, Arthur. Draw up that chair, and rest a little.'

'Thank you, Mrs – er – Mrs –?'

'Dolderson,' she told him.

'Thank you, Mrs Dolderson,' he said, frowning a little, trying to place the name.

She watched him pull the chair closer. Every movement, every line familiar, even to the lock of fair hair that always fell forward when he stooped. He sat down and remained silent for some moments, staring under a frown, across the garden.

Mrs Dolderson sat still, too. She was scarcely less bewildered than he, though she did not reveal it. Clearly the thought that she was dead had been quite silly. She was just as usual, still in her chair, still aware of the ache in her back, still able to grip the arms of the chair and feel them. Yet it was not a dream – everything was too textured, too solid, too real in a way that dream things never were. . . . Too sensible, too – that was, they would have been had the young man been any other than Arthur . . . ?

Was it just a simple hallucination? – A trick of her mind imposing Arthur's face on an entirely different young man?

She glanced at him. No, that would not do – he had

answered to Arthur's name. Indubitably he was Arthur – and wearing Arthur's blazer, too. . . . They did not cut them that way nowadays, and it was years and years since she had seen a young man wearing a straw hat . . . ?

A kind of ghost . . . ? But no – he was quite solid; the chair had creaked as he sat down, his shoes had crunched on the gravel. . . . Besides, whoever heard of a ghost in the form of a thoroughly bewildered young man, and one, moreover, who had recently nicked himself in shaving . . . ?

He cut her thoughts short by turning his head.

'I thought Thelma would be here,' he told her. 'She *said* she'd be here. Please tell me, where is she?'

Like a frightened little boy, she thought. She wanted to comfort him, not to frighten him more. But she could think of nothing to say beyond:

'Thelma isn't far away.'

'I must find her. She'll be able to tell me what's happened.' He made to get up.

She laid a hand on his arm, and pressed down gently.

'Wait a minute,' she told him. 'What is it that seems to have happened? What is it that worries you so much?'

'This,' he said, waving a hand to include everything about them. 'It's all different – and yet the same – and yet not . . . I feel as if – as if I'd gone a little mad.'

She looked at him steadily, and then shook her head.

'I don't think you have. Tell me, what is it that's wrong?'

'I was coming here to play tennis – well, to see Thelma really,' he amended. 'Everything was all right then – just as usual. I rode up the drive and leant my bike against the big fir tree where the path begins. I started to come along the path, and then, just when I reached the corner of the house, everything went funny. . . .'

'Went funny?' Mrs Dolderson inquired. 'What – went funny?'

'Well, nearly everything. The sun seemed to jerk in the sky. The trees suddenly looked bigger, and not quite the same. The flowers in the bed over there went quite a different colour.

This creeper which was all over the wall was suddenly only halfway up – and it looks like a different *kind* of creeper. And there are houses over there. I never saw them before – it's just an open field beyond the spinney. Even the gravel on the path looks more yellow than I thought. And this room. . . . It *is* the same room. I know that desk, and the fireplace – and those two pictures. But the paper is quite different. I've never seen that before – but it isn't new, either. . . . Please tell me where Thelma is . . . I want her to explain it . . . I *must* have gone a bit mad. . . .'

She put her hand on his, firmly.

'No,' she said decisively. 'Whatever it is, I'm quite sure it's not that.'

'Then what –?' He broke off abruptly, and listened, his head a little on one side. The sound grew. 'What is it?' he asked, anxiously.

Mrs Dolderson tightened her hand over his.

'It's all right,' she said, as if to a child. 'It's all right, Arthur.'

She could feel him grow tenser as the sound increased. It passed right overhead at less than a thousand feet, jets shrieking, leaving the buffeted air behind it rumbling back and forth, shuddering gradually back to peace.

Arthur saw it. Watched it disappear. His face when he turned it back to her was white and frightened. In a queer voice he asked:

'What – what was that?'

Quietly, as if to force calm upon him, she said:

'Just an aeroplane, Arthur. Such horrid, noisy things they are.'

He gazed where it had vanished, and shook his head.

'But I've *seen* an aeroplane, and *heard* it. It isn't like that. It makes a noise like a motor-bike, only louder. This was terrible! I don't understand – I don't understand what's happened. . . .' His voice was pathetic.

Mrs Dolderson made as if to reply, and then checked at a thought, a sudden sharp recollection of Harold talking about dimensions, of shifting them into different planes, speaking of time as though it were simply another dimension. . . . With a kind of shock of intuition she understood – no, understood was too firm a word – she perceived. But, perceiving, she found herself at a loss. She looked again at the young man. He was still tense, trembling slightly. He was wondering whether he was going out of his mind. She must stop that. There was no kind way – but how to be least unkind?

'Arthur,' she said, abruptly.

He turned a dazed look on her.

Deliberately she made her voice brisk.

'You'll find a bottle of brandy in that cupboard. Please fetch it – and two glasses,' she ordered.

With a kind of sleep-walking movement he obeyed. She filled a third of a tumbler with brandy for him, and poured a little for herself.

'Drink that,' she told him. He hesitated. 'Go on,' she commanded. 'You've had a shock. It will do you good. I want to talk to you, and I can't talk to you while you're knocked half-silly.'

He drank, coughed a little, and sat down again.

'Finish it,' she told him firmly. He finished it. Presently she inquired:

'Feeling better now?'

He nodded, but said nothing. She made up her mind, and drew breath carefully. Dropping the brisk tone altogether, she asked:

'Arthur. Tell me, what day is it today?'

'Day?' he said, in surprise. 'Why, it's Friday. It's the – er – twenty-seventh of June.'

'But the year, Arthur. What year?'

He turned his face fully towards her.

'I'm not *really* mad, you know. I know who I am, and where I am – I think. . . . It's *things* that have gone wrong, not me. I can tell you –'

'What I want you to tell me, Arthur, is the year.' The peremptory note was back in her voice again.

He kept his eyes steadily on hers as he spoke.

'Nineteen-thirteen, of course,' he said.

Mrs Dolderson's gaze went back to the lawn and the flowers. She nodded gently. That was the year – and it had been a Friday; odd that she should remember that. It might well have been the twenty-seventh of June. . . . But certainly a Friday in the summer of nineteen-thirteen was the day he had not come. . . . All so long, long ago. . . .

His voice recalled her. It was unsteady with anxiety.

'Why – why do you ask me that – about the year, I mean?'

His brow was so creased, his eyes so anxious. He was very young. Her heart ached for him. She put her thin fragile hand on his strong one again.

'I – I think I know,' he said shakily. 'It's – I don't see how, but you wouldn't have asked that unless. . . . That's the queer thing that's happened, isn't it? Somehow it isn't nineteen-thirteen any longer – that's what you mean? The way the trees grew . . . that aeroplane. . . .' He stopped, staring at her with wide eyes. 'You must tell me. . . . Please, please. . . . What's happened to me? – Where am I now? – Where is this . . . ?'

'My poor boy . . .' she murmured.

'Oh, please . . .'

The Times, with the crossword partly done, was pushed down into the chair beside her. She pulled it out half-reluctantly. Then she folded it over and held it towards him. His hand shook as he took it.

'London, Monday, the first of July,' he read. And then, in an incredulous whisper: '*Nineteen-sixty-three!*'

He lowered the page, looked at her imploringly.

She nodded twice, slowly.

They sat staring at one another without a word. Gradually, his expression changed. His brows came together, as though with pain. He looked round jerkily, his eyes darting here and there as if for an escape. Then they came back to her. He screwed them shut for a moment. Then opened them again, full of hurt – and fear.

'Oh, no – no . . . ! No . . . ! You're not. . . . You can't be. . .
You – you told me. . . . You're Mrs Dolderson, aren't you . . .
You said you were. . . . You can't – you can't be – Thelma . . . ?'

Mrs Dolderson said nothing. They gazed at one another.
His face creased up like a small child's.

'Oh, God! Oh – oh – oh . . . !' he cried, and hid his face
in his hands.

Mrs Dolderson's eyes closed for a moment. When they
opened she had control of herself again. Sadly she looked on
the shaking shoulders. Her thin, blue-veined left hand reached
out towards the bowed head, and stroked the fair hair, gently.

Her right hand found the bell-push on the table beside her.
She pressed it, and kept her finger upon it. . . .

At the sound of movement her eyes opened. The venetian
blind shaded the room but let in light enough for her to see
Harold standing beside her bed.

'I didn't mean to wake you, Mother,' he said.

'You didn't wake me, Harold. I was dreaming, but I was
not asleep. Sit down, my dear. I want to talk to you.'

'You mustn't tire yourself, Mother. You've had a bit of a
relapse, you know.'

'I dare say, but I find it more tiring to wonder than to know.
I shan't keep you long.'

'Very well, Mother.' He pulled a chair close to the bedside,
and sat down, taking her hand in his. She looked at his face in
the dimness.

'It was you who did it, wasn't it, Harold? It was that
experiment of yours that brought poor Arthur here?'

'It was an accident, Mother.'

'Tell me.'

'We were trying it out. Just a preliminary test. We knew
it was theoretically possible. We had shown that if we could –
oh, dear, it's so difficult to explain in words – if we could,
well, twist a dimension, kind of fold it back on itself, then two
points that are normally apart must coincide . . . I'm afraid
that's not very clear. . . .'

126

'Never mind, dear. Go on.'

'Well, when we had our field-distortion-generator fixed up we set it to bring together two points that are normally fifty years apart. Think of folding over a long strip of paper that has two marks on it, so that the marks are brought together.'

'Yes?'

'It was quite arbitrary. We might have chosen ten years, or a hundred, but we just picked on fifty. And we got astonishingly close, too, Mother, quite remarkably close. Only a four-day calendar error in fifty years. It's staggered us. The thing we've got to do now is to find out that source of error, but if you'd asked any of us to bet –'

'Yes, dear, I'm sure it was quite wonderful. But what *happened*?'

'Oh, sorry. Well, as I said, it was an accident. We only had the thing switched on for three or four seconds – and he must have walked slap into the field of coincidence right then. An outside – a millions-to-one chance. I wish it had not happened, but we couldn't possibly know. . . .'

She turned her head on the pillow.

'No. You couldn't know,' she agreed. 'And then?'

'Nothing, really. We didn't know until Jenny answered your bell to find you in a faint, and this chap, Arthur, all gone to pieces, and sent for me.

'One of the girls helped to get you to bed. Doctor Sole arrived, and took a look at you. Then he pumped some kind of tranquillizer into this Arthur. The poor fellow needed it, too – one hell of a thing to happen when all you were expecting was a game of tennis with your best girl.

'When he'd quietened down a bit he told us who he was, and where he'd come from. Well, there was a thing for you! Accidental living proof at the first shot.

'But all *he* wanted, poor devil, was to get back just as soon as he could. He was very distressed – quite a painful business. Doctor Sole wanted to put him right under to stop him cracking altogether. It looked that way, too – and it didn't look as if he'd be any better when he came round again, either.

'We didn't know if we *could* send him back. Transference "forward", to put it crudely, can be regarded as an infinite acceleration of a natural progression, but the idea of transference "back" is full of the most disconcerting implications once you start thinking about it. There was quite a bit of argument, but Doctor Sole clinched it. If there was a fair chance, he said, the chap had a right to try, and we had an obligation to try to undo what we'd done to him. Apart from that, if we did not try we should certainly have to explain to someone how we came to have a raving loony on our hands, and fifty years off course, so to speak.

'We tried to make it clear to this Arthur that we couldn't be sure that it would work in reverse – and that, anyway, there was this four-day calendar error, so at best it wouldn't be exact. I don't think he really grasped that. The poor fellow was in a wretched state; all he wanted was just a chance – any kind of chance – to get out of here. He was simply one-track.

'So we decided to take the risk – after all, if it turned out not to be possible he'd – well, he'd know nothing about it – or nothing would happen at all. . . .

'The generator was still on the same setting. We put one fellow on to that, took this Arthur back to the path by your room, and got him lined up there.

'"Now walk forward," we told him. "Just as you were walking when it happened." And we gave the switch-on signal. What with the doctor's dope and one thing and another he was pretty groggy, but he did his best to pull himself together. He went forward at a kind of stagger. Literal-minded fellow; he was half-crying, but in a queer sort of voice he was trying to sing: "Everybody's doin' it, do – "

'And then he disappeared – just vanished completely.' He paused, and added regretfully: 'All the evidence we have now is not very convincing – one tennis-racket, practically new, but vintage, and one straw-hat, ditto.'

Mrs Dolderson lay without speaking. He said:

'We did our best, Mother. We could only try.'

'Of course you did, dear. And you succeeded. It wasn't

your fault that you couldn't undo what you'd done. . . . No, I was just wondering what would have happened if it had been a few minutes earlier – or later, that you had switched your machine on. But I don't suppose that *could* have happened. . . . You wouldn't have been here at all if it had. . . .'

He regarded her a little uneasily.

'What *do* you mean, Mother?'

'Never mind, dear. It was, as you said, an accident. – At least, I suppose it was – though so many important things seem to be accidents that one does sometimes wonder if they aren't really *written* somewhere. . . .'

Harold looked at her, trying to make something of that, then he decided to ask:

'But what makes you think that we did succeed in getting him back, Mother?'

'Oh, I *know* you did, dear. For one thing I can very clearly remember the day I read in the paper that Lieutenant Arthur Waring Batley had been awarded a D.S.O. – some time in November nineteen-fifteen, I think it was.

'And, for another, I have just had a letter from your sister.'

'From Cynthia? How on earth does she come into it?'

'She wants to come and see us. She is thinking of getting married again, and she'd like to bring the young man – well, not such a very *young* man, I suppose – down here to show him.'

'That's all right, but I don't see –'

'She thinks you might find him interesting. He's a physicist.'

'But –'

Mrs Dolderson took no notice of the interruption. She went on:

'Cynthia tells me his name is Batley – and he's the son of a Colonel Arthur Waring Batley, D.S.O., of Nairobi, Kenya.'

'You mean, he's the son of –?'

'So it would seem, dear. Strange, isn't it?' She reflected a moment, and added: 'I must say that if these things *are* written, they do sometimes seem to be written in a very queerly distorted way, don't you think . . . ?'

E

Random Quest

The sound of a car coming to a stop on the gravel caused Dr Harshom to look at his watch. He closed the book in which he had been writing, put it away in one of his desk drawers, and waited. Presently Stephens opened the door to announce: 'Mr Trafford, sir.'

The doctor got up from his chair, and regarded the young man who entered, with some care. Mr Colin Trafford turned out to be presentable, just in his thirties, with brown hair curling slightly, clean-shaven, a suit of good tweed well cut, and shoes to accord. He looked pleasant enough though not distinguished. It would not be difficult to meet thirty or forty very similar young men in a day. But when he looked more closely, as the doctor now did, there were signs of fatigue to be seen, indications of anxiety in the expression and around the eyes, a strained doggedness in the set of the mouth.

They shook hands.

'You'll have had a long drive,' said the doctor. 'I expect you'd like a drink. Dinner won't be for half an hour yet.'

The younger man accepted, and sat down. Presently, he said:

'It was kind of you to invite me here, Dr Harshom.'

'Not really altruistic,' the doctor told him. 'It is more satisfactory to talk than to correspond by letter. Moreover, I am an inquisitive man recently retired from a very humdrum country practice, Mr Trafford, and on the rare occasions that I do catch the scent of a mystery my curiosity urges me to follow it up.' He, too, sat down.

'Mystery?' repeated the young man.

'Mystery,' said the doctor.

The young man took a sip of his whisky.

'My inquiry was such as one might receive from – well, from any solicitor,' he said.

'But you are not a solicitor, Mr Trafford.'

'No,' Colin Trafford admitted, 'I am not.'

'But you do have a very pressing reason for your inquiry. So there is the mystery. What pressing, or indeed leisurely, reason could you have for inquiries about a person whose existence you yourself appear to be uncertain – and of whom Somerset House has no record?'

The young man regarded him more carefully, as he went on:

'How do I know that? Because an inquiry there would be your natural first step. Had you found a birth-certificate, you would not have pursued the course you have. In fact, only a curiously determined person would have persisted in a quest for someone who had no official existence. So, I said to myself: When this persistence in the face of reason addresses itself to me I will try to resolve the mystery.'

The young man frowned.

'You imply that you said that *before* you had my letter?'

'My dear fellow, Harshom is not a common name – an unusual corruption of Harvesthome, if you are interested in such things – and, indeed, I never yet heard of a Harshom who was not traceably connected with the rest of us. And we do, to some extent, keep in touch. So, quite naturally, I think, the incursion of a young man entirely unknown to any of us, but persistently tackling us one after another with his inquiries regarding an unidentifiable Harshom, aroused our interest. Since it seemed that I myself came low on your priority list I decided to make a few inquiries of my own. I –'

'But why should you judge yourself low on a list,' Colin Trafford interrupted.

'Because you are clearly a man of method. In this case, geographical method. You began your inquiries with Harshoms in the Central London area, and worked outwards, until you are now in Herefordshire. There are only two further-flung

Harshoms now on your list, Peter, down in the toe of Cornwall, and Harold, a few miles from Durham – am I right?'

Colin Trafford nodded, with a trace of reluctance.

'You are,' he admitted.

Dr Harshom smiled, a trifle smugly.

'I thought so. There is –' he began, but the young man interrupted him again.

'When you answered my letter, you invited me here, but you evaded my question,' he remarked.

'That is true. But I have answered it now by insisting that the person you seek not only does not exist, but never did exist.'

'But if you're quite satisfied on that, why ask me here at all?'

'Because –' The doctor broke off at the sound of a gong. 'Dear me, Phillips allows one just ten minutes to wash. Let me show you your room, and we can continue over dinner.'

A little later when the soup was before them, he resumed:

'You were asking me why I invited you here. I think the answer is that since you feel entitled to be curious about a hypothetical relative of mine, I feel no less entitled to be curious about the motives that impel your curiosity. Fair enough? – as they say.'

'Dubious,' replied Mr Trafford after consideration. 'To inquire into my motives would, I admit, be not unreasonable if you knew this person to exist – but, since you assure me she does not exist, the question of my motives surely becomes academic.'

'My interest *is* academic, my dear fellow, but none the less real. Perhaps we might progress a little if I might put the problem as it appears from my point of view?'

Trafford nodded. The doctor went on:

'Well, now, this is the situation: Some seven or eight months ago a young man, unknown to any of us, begins a series of approaches to my relatives. His concern, he says, is to learn the whereabouts, or to gain any clues which may help him to trace the whereabouts of a lady called Ottilie Harshom. She was born, he believes, in 1928, though it could be a few years

133

to either side of that – and she may, of course, have adopted another surname through marriage.

'In his earlier letters there is an air of confidence suggesting his feeling that the matter will easily be dealt with, but as one Harshom after another fails to identify the subject of his inquiries his tone becomes less confident though not less determined. In one or two directions he does learn of young Harshom ladies – none of them called Ottilie, by the way, but he nevertheless investigates them with care. Can it be, perhaps, that he is as uncertain about the first name as about everything else concerning her? But apparently none of these ladies fulfils his requirements, for he presses on. In the face of unqualified unsuccess, his persistence in leaving no Harshom stone unturned begins to verge upon the unreasonable. Is he an eccentric, with a curious obsession?

'Yet by all the evidence he was – until the spring of 1953, at any rate, a perfectly normal young man. His full name is Colin Wayland Trafford. He was born in 1921, in Solihull, the son of a solicitor. He went to Chartowe School 1934. Enlisted in the Army 1939. Left it, with the rank of Captain 1945. Went up to Cambridge. Took a good degree in Physics 1949. Joined Electro-Physical Industries on the managerial side that same year. Married Della Stevens 1950. Became a widower 1951. Received injuries in a laboratory demonstration accident early in 1953. Spent the following five weeks in St Merryn's Hospital. Began his first approaches to members of the Harshom family for information regarding Ottilie Harshom about a month after his discharge from hospital.'

Colin Trafford said coldly:

'You are very fully informed, Dr Harshom.'

The doctor shrugged slightly.

'Your own information about the Harshoms must by now be almost exhaustive. Why should you resent some of us knowing something of you?'

Colin did not reply to that. He dropped his gaze, and appeared to study the tablecloth. The doctor resumed:

'I said just now – has he an obsession? The answer has

appeared to be yes – since some time last March. Prior to that, there seems to have been no inquiry whatever regarding Miss Ottilie Harshom.

'Now when I had reached this point I began to feel that I was on the edge of a more curious mystery than I had expected.' He paused. 'I'd like to ask you, Mr Trafford, had you ever been aware of the name Ottilie Harshom before January last?'

The young man hesitated. Then he said, uneasily:

'How can one possibly answer that? One encounters a myriad names on all sides. Some are remembered, some seem to get filed in the subconscious, some apparently fail to register at all. It's unanswerable.'

'Perhaps so. But we have the curious situation that before January Ottilie Harshom was apparently not on your mental map, but since March she has, without any objective existence, dominated it. So I ask myself, what happened between January and March . . . ?

'Well, I practise medicine. I have certain connexions, I am able to learn the external facts. One day late in January you were invited, along with several other people, to witness a demonstration in one of your Company's laboratories. I was not told the details, I doubt if I would understand them if I were: the atmosphere around the higher flights of modern physics is so rarefied – but I gather that during this demonstration something went amiss. There was an explosion, or an implosion, or perhaps a matter of a few atoms driven berserk by provocation, in any case, the place was wrecked. One man was killed outright, another died later, several were injured. You yourself were not badly hurt. You did get a few cuts, and bruises – nothing serious, but you were knocked out – right out. . . .

'You were, indeed, so thoroughly knocked out that you lay unconscious for twenty-four days. . . .

'And when at last you did come round you displayed symptoms of considerable confusion – more strongly, perhaps, than would be expected in a patient of your age and type, and you were given sedatives. The following night you slept restlessly, and showed signs of mental distress. In particular you called again and again for someone named Ottilie.

'The hospital made what inquiries they could, but none of your friends or relatives knew of anyone called Ottilie associated with you.

'You began to recover, but it was clear you had something heavily on your mind. You refused to reveal what it was, but you did ask one of the doctors whether he could have his secretary try to find the name Ottilie Harshom in any directory. When it could not be found, you became depressed. However, you did not raise the matter again – at least, I am told you did not – until after your discharge when you set out on this quest for Ottilie Harshom, in which, in spite of completely negative results, you continue.

'Now, what must one deduce from that?' He paused to look across the table at his guest, left eyebrow raised.

'That you are even better informed than I thought,' Colin said, without encouragement. 'If I were your patient your inquiries might be justified, but as I am not, and have not the least intention of consulting you professionally, I regard them as intrusive, and possibly unethical.'

If he had expected his host to be put out he was disappointed. The doctor continued to regard him with interested detachment.

'I'm not yet entirely convinced that you ought not to be someone's patient,' he remarked. 'However, let me tell you why it was I, rather than another Harshom, who was led to make these inquiries. Perhaps you may then think them less impertinent. But I am going to preface that with a warning against false hopes. You must understand that the Ottilie Harshom you are seeking *does not exist and has not existed.* That is quite definite.

'Nevertheless, there *is* one aspect of this matter which puzzled me greatly, and that I cannot bring myself to dismiss as coincidence. You see, the name Ottilie Harshom was not entirely unknown to me. No –' He raised his hand. '– I repeat, no false hopes. There *is no* Ottilie Harshom, but there has been – or, rather, there have in the past been, two Ottilie Harshoms.'

Colin Trafford's resentful manner had entirely dropped away. He sat, leaning a little forward, watching his host intently.

'But,' the doctor emphasized, 'it was all long ago. The first was my grandmother. She was born in 1832, married Grandfather Harshom in 1861, and died in 1866. The other was my sister: she, poor little thing, was born in 1884 and died in 1890. . . .'

He paused again. Colin made no comment. He went on:

'I am the only survivor of this branch so it is not altogether surprising that the others have forgotten there was ever such a name in the family, but when I heard of your inquiries I said to myself: There is something out of order here. Ottilie is not the rarest of names, but on any scale of popularity it would come a very long way down indeed; and Harshom *is* a rare name. The odds against these two being coupled by mere chance must be some quite astronomical figure. Something so large that I cannot believe it *is* chance. Somewhere there must be a link, some cause. . . .

'So, I set out to discover if I could find out why this young man Trafford should have hit upon this improbable conjunction of names – and, seemingly, become obsessed by it. – You would not care to help me at this point?'

Colin continued to look at him, but said nothing.

'No? Very well. When I had all the available data assembled the conclusion I had to draw was this: that as a result of your accident you underwent some kind of traumatic experience, an experience of considerable intensity as well as unusual quality. Its intensity one deduces from your subsequent fixation of purpose; the unusual quality partly from the pronounced state of confusion in which you regained consciousness, and partly from the consistency with which you deny recollecting anything from the moment of the accident until you awoke.

'Now, if that were indeed a blank, why did you awake in

such a confused condition? There must have been some recollection to cause it. And if there was something akin to ordinary dream images, why this refusal to speak of them? There must have been, therefore, some experience of great personal significance wherein the name Ottilie Harshom was a very potent element indeed.

'Well, Mr Trafford. Is the reasoning good, the conclusion valid? Let me suggest, as a physician, that such things are a burden that should be shared.'

Colin considered for some little time, but when he still did not speak the doctor added:

'You are almost at the end of the road, you know. Only two more Harshoms on the list, and I assure you they won't be able to help – so what then?'

Colin said, in a flat voice:

'I expect you are right. You should know. All the same, I must see them. There might be something, some clue. . . . I can't neglect the least possibility. . . . I had just a little hope when you invited me here. I knew that you had a family. . . .'

'I *had*,' the doctor said, quietly. 'My son Malcolm was killed racing at Brooklands in 1927. He was unmarried. My daughter married, but she had no children. She was killed in a raid on London in 1941. . . . So there it ends. . . .' He shook his head slowly.

'I am sorry,' said Colin. Then: 'Have you a picture of your daughter that I may see?'

'She wasn't of the generation you are looking for.'

'I realize that, but nevertheless. . . .'

'Very well – when we return to the study. Meanwhile, you've not yet said what you think of my reasoning.'

'Oh, it was good.'

'But you are still disinclined to talk about it? Well, I am not. And I can still go a little further. Now, this experience of yours cannot have been of a kind to cause a feeling of shame or disgust, or you would be trying to sublimate it in some way, which manifestly you are not. Therefore it is highly probable that the cause of your silence is fear. Something makes you afraid to discuss the experience. You are not, I am satisfied, afraid of facing it; therefore your fear must be of the consequences of communicating it. Consequences possibly to someone else, but much more probably to yourself. . . .'

Colin went on regarding him expressionlessly for a moment. Then he relaxed a little and leaned back in his chair. For the first time he smiled faintly.

'You do get there, in the end, don't you, Doctor? But do you mind if I say that you make quite Germanically heavy-going of it? And the whole thing is so simple, really. It boils down to this. If a man, any man, claims to have had an experience which is outside all normal experience, it will be inferred, will it not, that he is in some way not quite a normal man? In that case, he cannot be entirely relied upon to react to a particular situation as a normal man should – and if his reactions may be non-normal, how can he be really dependable? He may be, of course – but would it not be sounder policy to put authority into the hands of a man about whom there is *no* doubt? Better to be on the safe side. So he is passed over. His failure to make the expected step is not unnoticed. A small cloud, a mere wrack, of doubt and risk begins to gather above him. It is tenuous, too insubstantial for him to disperse, yet it casts a faint, persistent shadow.

'There is, I imagine, no such thing as a normal human being, but there is a widespread feeling that there ought to be. Any organization has a conception of "the type of man we want here" which is regarded as the normal for its purposes. So every man there attempts more or less to accord to it – organizational man, in fact – and anyone who diverges more than slightly from the type in either his public, or in his private life does so to the peril of his career. There is, as you said, fear of the results to myself: it is, as I said, so simple.'

'True enough,' the doctor agreed. 'But you have not taken any care to disguise the consequence of the experience – the hunt for Ottilie Harshom.'

'I don't need to. Could anything be more reassuringly normal than "man seeks girl"? I have invented a background which has quite satisfied any interested friends – and even several Harshoms.'

'I dare say. – None of them being aware of the "coincidence" in the conjunction of "Ottilie" with "Harshom". But I am.'

He waited for Colin Trafford to make some comment on that. When none came, he went on:

'Look, my boy. You have this business very heavily on your mind. There are only the two of us here. I have no links whatever with your firm. My profession should be enough safeguard for your confidence, but I will undertake a special guarantee if you like. It will do you good to unburden – and I should like to get to the bottom of this. . . .'

But Colin shook his head.

'You won't, you know. Even if I were to tell you, you'd only be the more mystified – as I am.'

'Two heads are better than one. We could try,' said the doctor, and waited.

Colin considered again, for some moments. Then he lifted his gaze, and met the doctor's steadily.

'Very well then. I've tried. You shall try. But first I would like to see a picture of your daughter. Have you one taken when she was about twenty-five?'

They left the table and went back to the study. The doctor waved Colin to a chair, and crossed to a corner cupboard. He took out a small pile of cardboard mounts and looked through them. He selected three, gazed at them thoughtfully for a few seconds, and then handed them over. While Colin studied them he busied himself with pouring brandy from a decanter.

Presently Colin looked up.

'No,' he said. 'And yet there is something. . . .' He tried covering parts of the full-face portrait with his hand. 'Something about the setting and shape of the eyes – but not quite. The brow, perhaps, but it's difficult to tell with the hair done like that. . . .' He pondered the photographs a little longer, and then handed them back. 'Thank you for letting me see them.'

The doctor picked up one of the others and passed it over.

'This was Malcolm, my son.'

It showed a laughing young man standing by the forepart of a car which bristled with exhaust manifold and had its bonnet held down by straps.

'He loved that car,' said the doctor, 'but it was too fast for the old track there. It went over the banking, and hit a tree.'

He took the picture back, and handed Colin a glass of brandy.

Colin swirled it. Neither of them spoke for some little time. Then he tasted the brandy, and, presently, lit a cigarette.

'Very well,' he said again. 'I'll try to tell you. But first I'll tell you what *happened* – whether it was subjective, or not, it happened for me. The implications and so on we can look at later – if you want to.'

'Good,' agreed the doctor. 'But tell me first, do we start from the moment of the accident – or was there anything at all relevant before that?'

'No,' Colin Trafford said, 'that's where it *does* start.'

It was just another day. Everything and everybody perfectly ordinary – except that this demonstration was something a bit special. What it concerned is not my secret, and not, as far as I know, relevant. We all gathered round the apparatus. Deakin who was in charge, pulled down a switch. Something began to hum, and then to whine, like a motor running faster and faster. The whine became a shriek as it went up the scale. There was a quite piercingly painful moment or two near the threshold of audibility, then a sense of relief because it was over and gone, with everything seeming quiet again. I was looking across at Deakin watching his dials, with his fingers held ready over the switches, and then, just as I was in the act of turning my head towards the demonstration again, there was a flash. . . . I didn't hear anything, or feel anything: there was just this dazzling white flash. . . . Then nothing but black. . . . I heard people crying out, and a woman's voice screaming . . . screaming . . . screaming. . . .

I felt crushed by a great weight. I opened my eyes. A sharp

pain jabbed through them into my head, but I struggled against the weight, and found it was due to two or three people being on top of me; so I managed to shove a couple of them off, and sit up. There were several other people lying about on the ground, and a few more picking themselves up. A couple of feet to my left was a large wheel. I looked farther up and found that it was attached to a bus – a bus that from my position seemed to tower like a scarlet skyscraper, and appeared, moreover, to be tilted and about to fall on me. It caused me to get up very quickly, and as I did I grabbed a young woman who had been lying across my legs, and dragged her to a safer place. Her face was dead white, and she was unconscious.

I looked around. It wasn't difficult to see what had happened. The bus, which must have been travelling at a fair speed, had, for some reason got out of control, run across the crowded pavement, and through the plate-glass window of a shop. The forepart of the top deck had been telescoped against the front of the building, and it was up there that the screaming was going on. Several people were still lying on the ground, a woman moving feebly, a man groaning, two or three more quite still. Three streams of blood were meandering slowly across the pavement among the crystals of broken glass. All the traffic had stopped, and I could see a couple of policemen's helmets bobbing through the crowd towards us.

I moved my arms and legs experimentally. They worked perfectly well, and painlessly. But I felt dazed, and my head throbbed. I put my hand up to it and discovered a quite tender spot where I must have taken a blow on the left occiput.

The policemen got through. One of them started pushing back the gaping bystanders, the other took a look at the casualties on the ground. A third appeared and went up to the top deck of the bus to investigate the screaming there.

I tried to conquer my daze, and looked round further. The place was Regent Street, a little up from Piccadilly Circus; the wrecked window was one of Austin Reed's. I looked up again at the bus. It was certainly tilted, but not in danger of toppling, for it was firmly wedged into the window opening to within a yard of the word 'General', gleaming in gold letters on its scarlet side.

At this point it occurred to me that I was supernumerary, and that if I were to hang around much longer I should find myself roped in as a witness – not, mind you, that I would grudge being a witness in the ordinary way, if it would do anyone any good, but I was suddenly and acutely aware that this was not at all in the ordinary way. For one thing I had no knowledge of anything whatever but the aftermath – and, for another, what was I doing here anyway. . . ? One moment I had been watching a demonstration out at Watford; the next, there was this. How the devil did I come to be in Regent Street at all. . . ?

I quietly edged my way into the crowd, then out of it again, zigzagged across the road amid the held-up traffic, and headed for the Café Royal, a bit further down.

They seemed to have done things to the old place since I was there last, a couple of years before, but the important thing was to find the bar, and that I did, without difficulty.

'A double brandy, and some soda,' I told the barman.

He gave it me, and slid along the siphon. I pulled some money out of my pocket, coppers and a little small silver. So I made to reach for my notecase.

'Half a crown, sir,' the barman told me, as if fending off a note.

I blinked at him. Still, he had said it. I slid over three shillings. He seemed gratified.

I added soda to the brandy, and took a welcome drink. It was as I was putting the glass down that I caught sight of myself in the mirror behind the bar. . . .

I used to have a moustache. I came out of the Army with it, but decided to jettison it when I went up to Cambridge. But there it was – a little less luxuriant, perhaps, but resurrected. I put up my hand and felt it. There was no illusion, and it was genuine, too. At almost the same moment I noticed my suit. Now, I used to have a suit pretty much like that,

143

years ago. Not at all a bad suit either, but still, not quite the thing we organization men wear in E.P.I. . . . .

I had a swimming sensation, took another drink of the brandy, and felt, a little unsteadily, for a cigarette. The packet I pulled out of my pocket was unfamiliar – have you ever heard of Player's 'Mariner' cigarettes – No? Neither had I, but I got one out, and lit it with a very unsteady match. The dazed feeling was not subsiding; it was growing, rapidly. . . .

I felt for my inside pocket. No wallet. It should have been there – perhaps some opportunist in the crowd round the bus had got it. . . . I sought through the other pockets – a fountain-pen, a bunch of keys, a couple of cash receipts from Harrods, a cheque book – containing cheques addressed to the Knights-bridge branch of the Westminster Bank. Well, the bank was all right, but why Knightsbridge? – I live in Hampstead. . . .

To try to get some kind of grip on things I began to recapitu-late from the moment I had opened my eyes and found the bus towering over me. It was quite vivid. I had a sharp recollection of staring up at that scarlet menace, with the gilded word 'General' shining brightly . . . yes, in gleaming gold – only, as you know, the word 'General' hasn't been seen on London buses since it was replaced by 'London Transport' in 1933. . . .

I was getting a little rattled by now, and looked round the bar for something to steady my wits. On one table I noticed a newspaper that someone had discarded. I went across to fetch it, and got carefully back on to my stool before I looked at it. Then I took a deep breath and regarded the front page. My first response was dismay for the whole thing was given up to a single display advertisement. Yet there was some reassurance, of a kind, at the top, for it read: '*Daily Mail*, London, Wednesday 27 January 1954.' So it was at least the right day – the one we had fixed for the demonstration at the labs.

I turned to the middle page, and read: 'Disorders in Delhi. One of the greatest exhibitions of civil disobedience so far staged in India took place here today demanding the immedi-ate release of Nehru from prison. For nearly all the hours of daylight the city has been at a standstill –' Then an item in an adjoining column caught my eye: 'In answer to a question from the Opposition front bench Mr Butler, the Prime Minister, assured the House that the Government was giving serious consideration –' In a dizzy way I glanced at the top of the page: the date there agreed with that on the front, 27 January 1954, but just below it there was a picture with the caption: 'A scene from last night's production of *The Lady Loves*, at the Laughton Theatre, in which Miss Amanda Coward plays the lead in the last of her father's many musical plays. *The Lady Loves* was completed only a few days before Noel Coward's death last August, and a moving tribute to his memory was paid at the end of the performance by Mr Ivor Novello who directed the production.'

I read that again, with care. Then I looked up and about, for reassurance, at my fellow drinkers, at the furniture, at the barman, at the bottles: it was all convincingly real.

I dropped the paper, and finished the rest of my brandy. I could have done with another, but it would have been awkward if, with my wallet gone, the barman should change his mind about his modest price. I glanced at my watch – and there was a thing, too! It was a very nice watch, gold, with a crocodile strap, and hands that stood at twelve-thirty, but I had never seen it before. I took it off and looked at the back. There was a pretty bit of engraving there; it said: 'C. for ever O. 10.x.50.' And it jolted me quite a little, for 1950 was the year I was married – though not in October, and not to anyone called O. My wife's name was Della. Mechanically I restrapped the watch on my wrist, and left.

The interlude and the brandy had done me some good. When I stepped out into Regent Street again I was feeling less dazed (though, if it is not too fine a distinction, more bewildered) and my head had almost ceased to ache, so that I was able to pay more attention to the world about me.

At first sight Piccadilly Circus gave an impression of being much as usual, and yet a suggestion that there was something a bit wrong with it. After a few moments I perceived that it was the people and the cars. Surprising numbers of the men and women, too, wore clothing that looked shabby, and the flower-girls below Eros seemed like bundles of rags. The look of the women who were not shabby took me completely aback. Almost without exception their hats were twelve-inch platter-like things balanced on the top of their heads. The skirts were long, almost to their ankles, and, worn under fur coats, gave an impression that they were dressed for the evening, at midday. Their shoes were pointed, over-ornamented, pin-heeled and quite hideous. I suppose all high-fashion would look ludicrous if one were to come upon it unprepared, but then one never does – at least one never had until now. . . . I might have felt like Rip van Winkle newly awakened, but for the date line on that newspaper. . . . The cars were odd, too. They seemed curiously high-built, small, and lacking in the flashy effects one had grown accustomed to, and when I paid more attention I did not see one make I could readily identify – except a couple of unmistakable Rolls.

While I stood staring curiously a plate-hatted lady in a well-worn fur-coat posted herself beside me and addressed me as 'dearie' in a somewhat grim way. I decided to move on, and headed for Piccadilly. On the way, I looked across at St James's Church. The last time I had seen it it was clothed in scaffolding, with a hoarding in the garden to help to raise funds for the rebuilding – that would have been about a fortnight before – but now all that had gone, and it looked as if it had never been bombed at all. I crossed the road to inspect it more closely, and was still more impressed with the wonderful job they had made of the restoration.

Presently I found myself in front of Hatchard's window, and paused to examine their contents. Some of the books had authors whose names I knew; I saw works by Priestley, C. S. Lewis, Bertrand Russell, T. S. Eliot, and others, but scarcely a title that I recognized. And then, down in the front, my eye was caught by a book in a predominantly pink jacket: *Life's Young Day*, a novel by Colin Trafford.

I went on goggling at it, probably with my mouth open.

I once had ambitions in that direction, you know. If it had not been for the war I'd probably have taken an Arts degree, and tried my hand at it, but as things happened I made a friend in the regiment who turned me to science, *and* could put me in the way of a job with E.P.I. later. Therefore it took me a minute or two to recover from the coincidence of seeing my name on the cover, and, when I did, my curiosity was still strong enough to take me into the shop.

There I discovered a pile of half a dozen copies lying on a table. I picked up the top one, and opened it. The name was plain enough on the title-page – and opposite was a list of seven other titles under 'author of'. I did not recognize the publisher's name, but overleaf there was the announcement: 'First published January 1954.'

I turned it over in my hand, and then all but dropped it. On the back was a picture of the author; undoubtedly me – and with the moustache. . . . The floor seemed to tilt slightly beneath my feet.

Then, somewhere over my shoulder, there was a voice; one that I seemed to recognize. It said:

'Well met, Narcissus! Doing a bit of sales-promotion, eh? How's it going?'

'Martin!' I exclaimed. I had never been so glad to see anyone in all my life. 'Martin. Why we've not met since – when was it?'

'Oh, for at least three days, old boy,' he said, looking a little surprised.

Three days! I'd seen a lot of Martin Falls at Cambridge, but only run across him twice since we came down, and the last of those was two years ago. But he went on:

'What about a spot of lunch, if you're not booked?' he suggested.

And that wasn't quite right either. I'd not heard anyone speak of a *spot* of lunch for years. However, I did my best to feel as if things were becoming more normal.

'Fine,' I said, 'but you'll have to pay. I've had my wallet pinched.'

He clicked his tongue.

'Hope there wasn't much in it. Anyway, what about the club? They'll cash you a cheque there.'

I put the book I was still holding back on the pile, and we left.

'Funny thing,' Martin said. 'Just run into Tommy – Tommy Westhouse. Sort of blowing sulphur – hopping mad with his American agent. You remember that god-awful thing of Tommy's – *The Thornèd Rose* – kind of Ben Hur meets Cleopatra, with the Marquis de Sade intervening? Well, it seems this agent –' He rambled on with a shoppy, anecdotal recital full of names that meant nothing to me, but lasted through several streets and brought us almost to Pall Mall. At the end of it he said: 'You didn't tell me how *Life's Young Day*'s doing. Somebody said it was over-subscribed. Saw the Lit. Sup. wagged a bit of a finger at you. Not had time to read it myself yet. Too much on hand.'

I chose the easier – the non-committal way. It seemed easier than trying to understand, so I told him it was doing just about as expected.

The Club, when in due course we reached it, turned out to be the Savage. I am not a member, but the porter greeted me by name, as though I were in the habit of dropping in every day.

'Just a quick one,' Martin suggested. 'Then we'll look in and see George about your cheque.'

I had misgivings over that, but it went off all right, and during lunch I did my best to keep my end up. I had the same troubles that I have now – true it was from the other end, but the principle still holds: if things are *too* queer people will find it easier to think you are potty than to help you; so keep up a front.

I am afraid I did not do very well. Several times I caught Martin glancing at me with a perplexed expression. Once he asked: 'Quite sure you're feeling all right, old man?'

But the climax did not come until, with cheese on his plate, he reached out his left hand for a stick of celery. And as he did so I noticed the gold signet ring on his little finger, and that jolted me right out of my caution – for, you see, Martin doesn't have a little finger on his left hand, or a third finger, either. He left both of them somewhere near the Rhine in 1945. . . .

'Good God!' I exclaimed. For some reason that pierced me more sharply than anything yet. He turned his face towards me.

'What on earth's the matter, man? You're as white as a sheet.'

'Your hand –' I said.

He glanced at it curiously, and then back at me, even more curiously.

'Looks all right to me,' he said, eyes a little narrowed.

'But – but you lost the two last fingers – in the war,' I exclaimed. His eyebrows rose, and then came down in an anxious frown. He said, with kind intention:

'Got it a bit mixed, haven't you, old man? Why, the war was over before I was born.'

Well, it goes a bit hazy just after that, and when it got coherent again I was lying back in a big chair, with Martin sitting close beside, saying:

'So take my advice, old man. Just you trot along to the quack this afternoon. Must've taken a bit more of a knock than you thought, you know. Funny thing, the brain – can't be too careful. Well, I'll have to go now I'm afraid. Appointment. But don't you put it off. Risky. Let me know how it goes.' And then he was gone.

I lay back in the chair. Curiously enough I was feeling far more myself than I had since I came to on the pavement in Regent Street. It was as if the biggest jolt yet had shaken me out of the daze, and got the gears of my wits into mesh again. . . . I was glad to be rid of Martin, and able to think. . . .

I looked round the lounge. As I said, I am not a member, and did not know the place well enough to be sure of details, but I rather thought the arrangement was a little different, and the carpet, and some of the light fittings, from when I saw it last. . . .

There were few people around. Two talking in a corner,

three napping, two more reading papers; none taking any notice of me. I went over to the periodicals table, and brought back the *New Statesman*, dated 22 January 1954. The front page leader was advocating the nationalization of transport as a first step towards putting the means of production into the hands of the people and so ending unemployment. There was a wave of nostalgia about that. I turned on, glancing at articles which baffled me for lack of context. I was glad to find Critic present, and I noticed that among the things that were currently causing him concern was some experimental work going on in Germany. His misgivings were, it seemed, shared by several eminent scientists, for, while there was little doubt now that nuclear fission was a theoretical possibility, the proposed methods of control were inadequate. There could well be a chain reaction resulting in a disaster of cosmic proportions. A consortium which included names famous in the Arts as well as many illustrious in the sciences was being formed to call upon the League of Nations to protest to the German government in the name of humanity against reckless research. . . .

Well, well . . . !

With returning confidence in myself I sat and pondered.

Gradually, and faintly at first, something began to glimmer. . . . Not anything about the how, or the why – I still have no useful theories about those – but about *what* could conceivably have happened.

It was vague – set off, perhaps, by the thought of that random neutron which I knew in one set of circumstances to have been captured by a uranium atom, but which, in another set of circumstances, apparently had not. . . .

And there, of course, one was brought up against Einstein and relativity which, as you know, denies the possibility of determining motion absolutely and consequently leads into the idea of the four-dimensional space-time continuum. Well, then, since you cannot determine the motions of the factors in the continuum, any pattern of motion must be illusory, and there cannot be any determinable consequences. Nevertheless, where the factors are closely similar – are composed of similar atoms in roughly the same relation to the continuum, so to speak – you *may* quite well get similar consequences. They can never be identical, of course, or determination of motion would be possible. But they could be very similar, and capable of consideration in terms of Einstein's Special Theory, and they *could* be determined further by a set of closely similar factors. In other words although the infinite point which we may call a moment in 1954 *must* occur throughout the continuum, it *exists* only in relation to each observer, and *appears* to have similar existence in relation to certain close groups of observers. However, since no two observers can be identical – that is, the same observer – each must perceive a different past, present, and future from that perceived by any other; consequently, what he perceives arises only from the factors of his relationship to the continuum, and exists only for him.

Therefore I began to understand that *what* had happened must be this: in some way – which I cannot begin to grasp – I had somehow been translated to the position of a different observer – one whose angle of view was in some respects very close to my own, and yet different enough to have relationships, and therefore realities, unperceived by me. In other words, he must have lived in a world real only to him, just as I had lived in a world real only to me – until this very peculiar transposition had occurred to put me in the position of observing *his* world, with, of course, its relevant past and future, instead of the one I was accustomed to.

Mind you, simple as it is when you consider it, I certainly did not grasp the form of it all at once, but I did argue my way close enough to the observer-existence relationship to decide that whatever might have gone amiss, my own mind was more or less all right. The trouble really seemed to be that it was in the wrong place, and getting messages not intended for me; a receiver somehow hooked into the wrong circuit.

Well, that's not good, in fact, it's bad; but it's still a lot better than a faulty receiver. And it braced me a bit to realize that.

I sat there quite a time trying to get it clear, and wondering what I should do, until I came to the end of my packet of 'Mariner' cigarettes. Then I went to the telephone.

First I dialled Electro-Physical Industries. Nothing happened. I looked them up in the book. It was quite a different number, on a different exchange. So I dialled that.

'Extension one three three,' I told the girl on the desk, and then, on second thoughts, named my own department.

'Oh. You want Extension five nine,' she told me.

Somebody answered. I said:

'I'd like to speak to Mr Colin Trafford.'

'I'm sorry. We've no one of that name in this department,' the voice told me.

Back to the desk. Then a longish pause.

'I'm sorry,' said the girl. 'I can't find that name on our staff list.'

I hung up. So, evidently, I was not employed by E.P.I. I thought a moment, and then dialled my Hampstead number. It answered promptly. 'Transcendental Belts and Corsets,' it announced brightly. I put down the receiver.

It occurred to me to look myself up in the book. I was there, all right: 'Trafford, Colin W., 54 Hogarth Court, Duchess Gardens, sw7. SLOane 67021.' So I tried that. The phone at the other end rang . . . and went on ringing. . . .

I came out of the box wondering what to do next. It was an extremely odd feeling to be bereft of orientation, rather as if one had been dropped abruptly into a foreign city without even a hotel room for a base – and somehow made worse by the city being foreign only in minor and personal details.

After further reflection I decided that the best protective colouration would come from doing what *this* Colin Trafford might reasonably be expected to do. If he had no work to do at E.P.I., he did at least have a home to go to. . . .

A nice block of flats, Hogarth Court, springy carpet and illuminated floral arrangement in the hall, that sort of thing, but, at the moment no porter in view, so I went straight to the lift. The place did not look big enough to contain fifty-four flats, so I took a chance on the five meaning the fifth floor, and sure enough I stepped out to find 54 on the door facing me. I took out my bunch of keys, tried the most likely one, and it fitted.

Inside was a small hall. Nothing distinctive – white paint, lightly patterned paper, close maroon carpet, occasional table with telephone and a few flowers in a vase, with a nice gilt-framed mirror above, the hard occasional chair, a passage off, lots of doors. I paused.

'Hullo,' I said, experimentally. Then a little louder: 'Hullo! Anyone at home?'

Neither voice nor sound responded. I closed the door behind me. What now? Well – well, hang it, I was – am – Colin Trafford! I took off my overcoat. Nowhere to put it. Second try revealed the coat closet. . . . Several other coats already in there. Male and female, a woman's overshoes, too. . . . I added mine.

I decided to get the geography of the place, and see what home was really like. . . .

Well, you won't want an inventory, but it was a nice flat. Larger than I had thought at first. Well furnished and arranged; not with extravagance, but not with stint, either. It showed taste, too; though not my taste – but what is taste? Either feeling for period, or refined selection from a fashion. I could feel that this was the latter, but the fashion was strange to me, and therefore lacked attraction. . . .

The kitchen was interesting. A fridge, no washer, single-sink, no plate racks, no laminated tops, old-fashioned-looking electric cooker, packet of soap powder, no synthetic detergents, curious lighting panel about three feet square in the ceiling, no mixer. . . .

The sitting-room was airy, chairs comfortable. Nothing spindly. A large radiogram, rather ornate, no F.M. on its scale. Lighting again by ceiling panels, and square things like glass cake-boxes on stands. No television.

I prowled round the whole place. Bedroom feminine, but not fussy. Twin beds. Bathroom tiled, white. Spare bedroom, small double-bed. And so on. But it was a room at the end of the passage that interested me most. A sort of study. One wall all bookshelves, some of the books familiar – the older ones – others not. An easy-chair, a lighter chair. In front of the window a broad, leather-topped desk, with a view across the bare-branched trees in the Gardens, roofs beyond, plenty of sky. On the desk a covered typewriter, adjustable lamp, several folders with sheets of paper untidily projecting, cigarette box, metal ash-tray, clean and empty, and a photograph in a leather frame.

I looked at the photograph carefully. A charming study. She'd be perhaps twenty-four – twenty-five? Intelligent, happy-looking, somebody one would like to know – but not anyone I did know. . . .

There was a cupboard on the left of the desk, and, on it, a glass-fronted case with eight books in it; the rest was empty. The books were all in bright paper jackets, looking as new. The one on the right-hand end was the same that I had seen in Hatchard's that morning – *Life's Young Day*; all the rest, too, bore the name Colin Trafford. I sat down in the swivel chair at the desk and pondered them for some moments. Then, with a curious, schizoid feeling I pulled out *Life's Young Day*, and opened it.

It was, perhaps, half an hour, or more, later that I caught the sound of a key in the outer door. I laid down the book, and thought rapidly. I decided that, on the whole, it would be better to disclose myself than wait to be discovered. So I opened the door. Along at the end of the passage a figure in a three-quarter length grey suède coat which showed a tweed skirt beneath was dumping parcels on to the hall table. At the sound of my door she turned her head. It was the original of the photograph, all right; but not in the mood of the photograph. As I approached, she looked at me with an expression of surprise, mixed with other feelings that I could not identify; but certainly it was not an adoring-wife-greets-devoted-husband look.

'Oh,' she said. 'You're in. What happened?'

'Happened?' I repeated, feeling for a lead.

'Well, I understood you had one of those so-important meetings with Dickie at the B.B.C. fixed for this afternoon,' she said, a little curtly I thought.

'Oh. Oh, that, yes. Yes, he had to put it off,' I replied, clumsily.

She stopped still, and inspected me carefully. A little oddly, too, I thought. I stood looking at her, wondering what to do, and wishing I had had the sense to think up some kind of plan for this inevitable meeting instead of wasting my time over *Life's Young Day*. I hadn't even had the sense to find out her name. It was clear that I'd got away wrong somehow the moment I opened my mouth. Besides, there was a quality about her that upset my balance altogether. . . . It hit me in a way I'd not known for years, and more shrewdly than it had then. . . . Somehow, when you are thirty-three you don't expect these things to happen – well, not to happen quite like that, any more. . . . Not with a great surge in your heart, and everything coming suddenly bright and alive as if she had just switched it all into existence. . . .

So we stood looking at one another; she with a half-frown, I trying to cope with a turmoil of elation and confusion, unable to say a word.

She glanced down, and began to unbutton her coat. She, too, seemed uncertain.

'If –' she began. But at that moment the telephone rang.

With an air of welcoming the interruption, she picked up the receiver. In the quiet of the hall I could hear a woman's voice ask for Colin.

'Yes,' she said, 'he's here.' And she held the receiver out to me, with a very curious look.

'Hullo,' I said. 'Colin here.'

'Oh, indeed,' replied the voice, 'and why, may I ask?'

'Er – I don't quite –' I began, but she cut me short.

'Now, look here, Colin, I've already wasted an hour waiting for you, thinking that if you couldn't come you might at least have had the decency to ring me up and tell me. Now I find you're just sitting at home. Not quite good enough, Colin.'

'I – um – Who is it? Who's speaking?' was the only temporizing move I could think of. I was acutely conscious that the young woman beside me was frozen stock-still in the act of taking off her coat.

'Oh, for God's sake,' said the voice, exasperated. 'What silly game is this? Who do you *think* it is?'

'That's what I'm asking,' I said.

'Oh, don't be such a clown, Colin. If it's because Ottilie's still there – and I bet she is – you're just being stupid. She answered the phone herself, so she *knows* it's me.'

'Then perhaps I'd better ask her who you are,' I suggested.

'Oh – you must be tight as an owl. Go and sleep it off,' she snapped, and the phone went dead.

I put the receiver back in the rest. The young woman was looking at me with an expression of genuine bewilderment. In the quietness of the hall she must have been able to hear the other voice almost as clearly as I had. She turned away, and busied herself with taking her coat off and putting it on a hanger in the closet. When she'd carefully done that she turned back.

'I don't understand,' she said. 'You aren't tight, are you? What's it all about? What has dear Dickie done?'

'Dickie?' I inquired. The slight furrow between her brows deepened.

'Oh, really, Colin. If you think I don't know Dickie's voice on the telephone by this time . . .'

'Oh,' I said. A bloomer of a peculiarly cardinal kind, that. In fact, it is hard to think of a more unlikely mistake than that a man should confuse the gender of his friends. Unless I wanted to be thought quite potty, I must take steps to clarify the situation.

'Look, can't we go into the sitting-room. There's something I want to tell you,' I suggested.

She watched me thoughtfully.

'I think perhaps I'd rather not hear it, Colin.'

'Please,' I said. 'It's important. It really is. . . .'

She hesitated, and then consented, reluctantly.

'Oh, very well, if you must. . . .'

We went in. She switched on the heater, and sat down. 'Well?' she asked.

I took the chair opposite, and wondered how to begin. Even if I had been clear in my own mind about what had happened, it would have been difficult enough. But how to convey that though the physical form was Colin Trafford's, and I myself was Colin Trafford, yet I was not *that* Colin Trafford; not the one who writes books and was married to her, but a kind of alternative Colin Trafford astray from an alternative world? What seemed to be wanted was some kind of approach which would not immediately suggest a call for an alienist – and it wasn't easy to perceive.

'Well?' she repeated.

'It's difficult to explain,' I temporized, but truthfully enough.

'I'm sure it is,' she replied, without encouragement, and added: 'Would it perhaps be easier if you didn't look at me like that? I'd prefer it, too.'

'Something very odd has happened to me,' I told her.

'Oh dear, again?' she said. 'Do you want my sympathy, or something?'

I was taken aback, and a little confused.

'Do you mean it's happened to him before?' I asked.

She looked at me hard.

'Him? Who's him? I thought you were talking about you. And what I mean is last time it happened it was Dickie, and the time before that it was Frances, and before that it was Lucy. . . . And now you've given Dickie a most peculiar kind of brush-off. . . . Am I supposed to be surprised. . . ?'

I was learning about my *alter ego* quite fast, but we were off the track. I tried:

'No, you don't understand. This is something quite different.'

'Of course not. Wives never do, do they? And it's always different. Well, if that's all that's so important. . . .' She began to get up.

'No, please . . .' I said anxiously.

She checked herself, looking very carefully at me again. The half-frown came back.

'No,' she said. 'No, I don't think I do understand. At least, I – I hope not. . . .' And she went on examining me, with something like growing uncertainty, I thought.

When you plead for understanding you can scarcely keep it on an impersonal basis, but when you don't know whether the best address would be 'my dear,' or 'darling,' or some more intimate variant, nor whether it should be prefaced by first name, nickname, or pet name, the way ahead becomes thorny indeed. Besides, there was this persistent misunderstanding on the wrong level.

'Ottilie, darling,' I tried – and that was clearly no usual form, for, momentarily, her eyes almost goggled, but I ploughed on: 'It isn't at all what you're thinking – nothing a bit like that. It's – well, it's that in a way I'm not the same person. . . .'

She was back in charge of herself.

'Oddly enough, I've been aware of that for some time,' she said. '*And* I could remind you that you've said something like that before, more than once. All right then, let me go on for you; so you're not the same person I married, so you'd like a divorce – or is it that you're afraid Dickie's husband is going to cite you this time? Oh, God! How sick I am of all this. . . .'

'No, no,' I protested desperately. 'It's not that sort of thing at all. Do please be patient. It's a thing that's terribly difficult to explain. . . .' I paused, looking at her. That did not make it any easier. Indeed, it was far from helping the rational processes. She sat looking back at me, still with that half-frown, but now it was a little more uneasy than displeased.

'Something *has* happened to you . . .' she said.

'That's what I'm trying to tell you about,' I told her, but I doubt whether she heard it. Her eyes grew wider as she looked. Suddenly they avoided mine.

'No!' she said. 'Oh, *no*!' She looked as if she were about

to cry, and wound her fingers tightly together in her lap. She half-whispered: 'Oh, no! . . . Oh, please God, no! . . . Not again. . . . Haven't I been hurt enough? . . . I won't . . . I won't . . . !'

Then she jumped up, and, before I was half-way out of my chair, she was out of the room. . . .

Colin Trafford paused to light a fresh cigarette, and took his time before going on. At length he pulled his thoughts back.

'Well,' he went on, 'obviously you will have realized by now that *that* Mrs Trafford was born Ottilie Harshom. It happened in 1928, and she married *that* Colin Trafford in 1949. Her father was killed in a plane crash in 1938 – I don't remember her ever mentioning his first name. That's unfortunate – there are a lot of things that are unfortunate: had I had any idea that I might be jerked back here I'd have taken more notice of a lot of things. But I hadn't. . . . Something exceedingly odd had happened, but that was no reason to suppose that an equally odd thing would happen, in reverse. . . .

'I did do my best, out of my own curiosity, to discover when the schism had taken place. There must, as I saw it, have been some point where, perhaps by chance, some pivotal thing had happened, or failed to happen, and finding it could bring one closer to knowing the moment, the atom of time, that had been split by some random neutron to give two atoms of time diverging into different futures. Once that had taken place, consequences gradually accumulating would make the conditions on one plane progressively different from those on the other.

'Perhaps that is always happening. Perhaps chance is continually causing two different outcomes so that in a dimension we cannot perceive there are infinite numbers of planes, some so close to our own and so recently split off that they vary only in minor details, others vastly different. Planes on which some misadventure caused Alexander to be beaten by the Persians, Scipio to fall before Hannibal, Caesar to stay beyond the Rubicon; infinite, infinite planes of the random split and re-split by the random. Who can tell? But, now that we know the Universe for a random place, why not?

'But I couldn't come near fixing the moment. It was, I *think*, somewhere in late 1926, or early 1927. Further than that one seemed unable to go without the impossible data of quantities of records from both planes for comparison. Something happening, or not happening, about then had brought about results which prevented, among other things, the rise of Hitler, and thus the Second World War – and consequently postponed the achievement of nuclear fission on this plane of our dichotomy – if that is a good word for it.

'Anyway, it was for me, and as I said, simply a matter of incidental curiosity. My active concerns were more immediate. And the really important one was Ottilie. . . .

'I have, as you know, been married – and I was fond of my wife. It was, as people say, a successful marriage, and it never occurred to me to doubt that – until this thing happened to me. I don't want to be disloyal to Della now, and I don't think she was unhappy – but I am immensely thankful for one thing: that this did not happen while she was alive; she never knew, because I didn't know then, that I had married the wrong woman – and I hope she never thought it. . . .

'And Ottilie had married the wrong man. . . . We found that out. Or perhaps one should put it that she had not married the man she thought she had. She had fallen in love with him; and, no doubt, he had loved her, to begin with – but in less than a year she became torn between the part she loved, and the side she detested. . . .

'Her Colin Trafford looked like me – right down to the left thumb which had got mixed up in an electric fan and never quite matched the other side – indeed, up to a point, that point somewhere in 1926–7 he *was* me. We had, I gathered, some mannerisms in common, and voices that were similar – though we differed in our emphases, and in our vocabularies, as I learnt from a tape, and in details: the moustache, the way we wore our hair, the scar on the left side of the forehead which was exclusively his, yet, in a sense, I was him and he was me. We had the same parents, the same genes, the same beginning, and – if I was right about the time of the dichotomy – we must have had the same memory of our life, for the first five years or so.

'But, later on, things on our different planes must have run differently for us. Environment, or experiences, had developed qualities in him which, I have to think, lie latent in me – and, I suppose, vice versa.

'I think that's a reasonable assumption, don't you? After all, one begins life with a kind of armature which has individual differences and tendencies, though a common general plan, but whatever is modelled on that armature later consists almost entirely of stuff from contacts and influences. What these had been for the other Colin Trafford I don't know, but I found the results somewhat painful – rather like continually glimpsing oneself in unexpected distorting mirrors.

'There were certain cautions, restraints, and expectations in Ottilie that taught me a number of things about him, too. Moreover, in the next day or two I read his novels attentively. The earliest was not displeasing, but as the dates grew later, and the touch surer I cared less and less for the flavour; no doubt the widening streaks of brutality showed the calculated development of a selling-point, but there was something a little more than that – besides, one has a choice of selling-points. . . . With each book I resented seeing my name on the title-page a little more.

'I discovered the current "work in progress" too. With the help of his notes I could, I believe, have produced a passable forgery, but I knew I would not. If I had to continue his literary career, it would be with my kind of books, not his. But, in any case, I had no need to worry over making a living: what with the war and one thing and another, physics on my own plane was a generation ahead of theirs. Even if they had got as far as radar it was still someone's military secret. I had enough knowledge to pass for a genius, and make my fortune if I cared to use it. . . .'

He smiled, and shook his head. He went on:

'You see, once the first shock was over and I had begun to perceive what must have happened, there was no cause for alarm, and, once I had met Ottilie, none for regret. The only problem was adjustment. It helped in general, I found, to try to get back to as much as I could remember of the pre-war world. But details were more difficult: unrecognized friends, lapsed friends, all with unknown histories, some of them with wives, or husbands, I knew (though not necessarily the same ones); some with quite unexpected partners. There were queer moments, too – an encounter with a burly cheerful man in the the bar of the Hyde Park Hotel. He didn't know me, but I knew him; the last time I had seen him he was lying by a road with a sniper's bullet through his head. I saw Della, my wife, leaving a restaurant looking happy, with her arm through that of a tall legal-looking type; it was uncanny to have her glance at me as at a complete stranger – I felt as if both of us were ghosts – but I was glad she had got past 1951 all right on that plane. The most awkward part was frequently running into people that it appeared I should know; the other Colin's acquaintanceship was evidently vast and curious. I began to favour the idea of proclaiming a breakdown from overwork, to tide me over for a bit.

'One thing that did not cross my mind was the possibility of what I took to be a unique shift of plane occurring again, this time in reverse. . . .

'– I am thankful it did not. It would have blighted the three most wonderful weeks in my life. I thought it was, as the engraving on the back of the watch said: "C. for ever O."

'I made a tentative attempt to explain to her what I thought had happened, but it wasn't meaning anything to her, so I gave it up. I think she had it worked out for herself that somewhere about a year after we were married I had begun to suffer from overstrain, and that now I had got better and become again the kind of man she had thought I was . . . something like that . . . but theories about it did not interest her much – it was the consequence that mattered. . . .

'And how right she was – for me, too. After all, what else

162

did matter? As far as I was concerned, nothing. I was in love. What did it matter *how* I had found the one unknown woman I had sought all my life. I was happy, as I had never expected to be. . . . Oh, all the phrases are trite, but "on top of the world" was suddenly, half-ridiculously vivid. I was full of a confidence rather like that of the slightly drunk. I could take anything on. With her beside me I could keep on top of that, or any, world. . . . I think she felt like that, too. I'm sure she did. She'd wiped out the bad years. Her faith was re-growing, stronger every day. . . . If I'd only known – but how could I know? What could I do . . . ?'

Again he stopped talking, and stared into the fire, this time for so long that at last the doctor fidgeted in his chair to recall him, and then added:

'What happened?'

Colin Trafford still had a faraway look.

'Happened?' he repeated. 'If I knew that I could perhaps – but I *don't* know. . . . There's nothing *to* know. . . . *It's* random, too. . . . One night I went to sleep with Ottilie beside me – in the morning I woke up in a hospital bed – back here again. . . . That's all there was to it. All there is. . . . Just random. . . .'

In the long interval that followed, Dr Harshom unhurriedly refilled his pipe, lit it with careful attention, assured himself it was burning evenly and drawing well, settled himself back comfortably, and then said, with intentional matter-of-factness:

'It's a pity you don't believe that. If you did, you'd never have begun this search; if you'd come to believe it, you'd have dropped the search before now. No, you believe that there is a pattern or rather, that there were two patterns, closely similar to begin with, but gradually, perhaps logically, becoming more variant – and that you, your psyche, or whatever you like to call it, was the aberrant, the random factor.

'However, let's not go into the philosophical, or metaphysical consideration of what you call the dichotomy now – all that stuff will keep. Let us say that I accept the validity of your experience, for you, but reserve judgement on its nature.

I accept it on account of several features – not the least being, as I have said, the astronomical odds against the conjunction of names, Ottilie and Harshom, occurring fortuitously. Of course, you *could* have seen the name somewhere and lodged it in your subconscious, but that, too, I find so immensely improbable that I put it aside.

'Very well, then, let us go on from there. Now, you appear to me to have made a number of quite unwarrantable assumptions. You have assumed, for instance, that because an Ottilie Harshom exists on what you call *that* plane, she must have come into existence on this plane also. I cannot see that that is justified by anything you have told me. That she *might* have existed here, I admit, for the name Ottilie is in my branch of the family; but the chances of her having no existence at all are considerably greater – did not you yourself mention that you recognized friends who in different circumstances were married to different wives? – is it not, therefore, highly probable that the circumstances which produced an Ottilie Harshom there failed to occur here, with the result that she could not come into existence at all? And, indeed, that must be so.

'Believe me, I am not unsympathetic. I do understand what your feelings must be, but are you not, in effect, in the state we all have known – searching for an ideal young woman who has never been born? We must face the facts: if she exists, or did exist, I should have heard of her, Somerset House would have a record of her, your own extensive researches would have revealed *something* positive. I do urge you for your own good to accept it, my boy. With all this against you, you simply have no case.'

'Only my own positive conviction,' Colin put in. 'It's against reason, I know – but I still have it.'

'You must try to rid yourself of it. Don't you see there are layers of assumptions? If she did exist she might be already married.'

'But to the wrong man,' Colin said promptly.

'Even that does not follow. Your counterpart varied from you, you say. Well, her counterpart if she existed would have had an entirely different upbringing in different circumstances from the other; the probability is that there would only be the most superficial resemblance. You must see that the whole thing goes into holes wherever you touch it with reason.' He regarded Colin for a moment, and shook his head. 'Somewhere at the back of your mind you are giving house-room to the proposition that unlike causes can produce like results. Throw it out.'

Colin smiled.

'How Newtonian, Doctor. No, a random factor is random. Chance therefore exists.'

'Young man, you're incorrigible,' the doctor told him. 'If there weren't little point in wishing success with the impossible I'd say your tenacity deserves it. As things are, I advise you to apply it to the almost attainable.'

His pipe had gone out, and he lit it again.

'That,' he went on, 'was a professional recommendation. But now, if it isn't too late for you, I'd like to hear more. I don't pretend to guess at the true nature of your experience, but the speculations your plane of might-have-been arouses are fascinating. Not unnaturally one feels a curiosity to know how one's own counterpart made out there – and failing that, how other people's did. Our present Prime Minister, for instance – did both of him get the job? And Sir Winston – or is he not *Sir* Winston over there? – how on earth did he get along with no Second World War to make his talents burgeon? And what about the poor old Labour Party. . . ? The thing provokes endless questions. . . .'

After a late breakfast the next morning Dr Harshom helped Colin into his coat in the hall, but held him there for a final word.

'I spent what was left of the night thinking about this,' he said earnestly. 'Whatever the explanation may be, you must write it down, every detail you can remember. Do it anonymously if you like, but do it. It may not be unique, some day it may give valuable confirmation of someone else's experience, or become evidence in support of some theory. So put it on record – but then leave it at that. . . . Do your best to forget the assumptions you jumped at – they're unwarranted in a dozen ways. *She does not exist.* The only Ottilie Harshoms there have been in this world died long ago. Let the mirage fade. But thank you for your confidence. Though I am inquisitive, I am discreet. If there should be any way I can help you. . . .'

Presently he was watching the car down the drive. Colin waved a hand just before it disappeared round the corner. Dr Harshom shook his head. He knew he might as well have saved his breath, but he felt in duty bound to make one last appeal. Then he turned back into the house, frowning. Whether the obsession was a fantasy, or something more than a fantasy, was almost irrelevant to the fact that sooner or later the young man was going to drive himself into a breakdown. . . .

During the next few weeks Dr Harshom learnt no more, except that Colin Trafford had not taken his advice, for word filtered through that both Peter Harshom in Cornwall and Harold in Durham had received requests for information regarding a Miss Ottilie Harshom who, as far as they knew, was non-existent.

After that there was nothing more for some months. Then a picture-postcard from Canada. On one side was a picture of the Parliament Buildings, Ottawa. The message on the other was brief. It said simply:

'Found her. Congratulate me. C.T.'

Dr Harshom studied it for a moment, and then smiled slightly. He was pleased. He had thought Colin Trafford a likeable young man; too good to run himself to pieces over such a futile quest. One did not believe it for a moment, of course, but if some sensible young woman had managed to convince him that she was the reincarnation, so to speak, of his beloved, good luck to her – and good luck for him. . . . The obsession could now fade quietly away. He would have liked to respond with the requested congratulations, but the card bore no address.

Several weeks later there was another card, with a picture of St Mark's Square, Venice. The message was again laconic, but headed this time by an hotel address. It read:

'Honeymoon. May I bring her to see you after?'

Dr Harshom hesitated. His professional inclination was against it; a feeling that anything likely to recall the young man to the mood in which he had last seen him was best avoided. On the other hand, a refusal would seem odd as well as rude. In the end he replied, on the back of a picture of Hereford Cathedral:

'Do. When?'

Half August had already gone before Colin Trafford did make his reappearance. He drove up looking sunburnt and in better shape all round than he had on his previous visit. Dr Harshom was glad to see it, but surprised to find that he was alone in the car.

'But I understood the whole intention was that I should meet the bride,' he protested.

'It was – it is,' Colin assured him. 'She's at the hotel. I – well, I'd like to have a few words with you first.'

The doctor's gaze became a little keener, his manner more thoughtful.

'Very well. Let's go indoors. If there's anything I'm not to mention, you could have warned me by letter, you know.'

'Oh, it's not that. She knows about that. Quite what she makes of it, I'm not sure, but she knows, and she's anxious to meet you. No, it's – well, it won't take more than ten minutes.'

The doctor led the way to his study. He waved Colin to an easy-chair, and himself took the swivel-chair at the desk.

'Unburden yourself,' he invited.

Colin sat forward, forearms on knees, hands dangling between them.

'The most important thing, Doctor, is for me to thank you.

167

I can never be grateful enough to you – never. If you had not invited me here as you did, I think it is unlikely I would ever have found her.'

Dr Harshom frowned. He was not convinced that the thanks were justified. Clearly, whoever Colin had found was possessed of a strong therapeutic quality, nevertheless:

'As I recollect, all I did was listen, and offer you unwelcome advice for your own good – which you did not take,' he remarked.

'So it seemed to me at the time,' Colin agreed. 'It looked as if you had closed all the doors. But when, then I thought it over, I saw one, just one, that hadn't quite latched.'

'I don't recall giving you *any* encouragement,' Dr Harshom asserted.

'I am sure you don't but you did. You indicated to me the last, faintly possible line – and I followed it up – No, you'll see what it was later, if you'll just bear with me a little.

'When I did see the possibility, I realized it meant a lot of ground-work that I couldn't cover on my own, so I had to call in the professionals. They were pretty good, I thought, and they certainly removed any doubt about the line being the right one, but what they could tell me ended on board a ship bound for Canada. So then I had to call in some inquiry agents over there. It's a large country. A lot of people go to it. There was a great deal of routine searching to do, and I began to get discouraged, but then they got a lead, and in another week they came across with the information that she was a secretary working in a lawyer's office in Ottawa.

'Then I put it to E.P.I. that I'd be more valuable after a bit of unpaid recuperative leave –'

'Just a minute,' put in the doctor. 'If you'd asked me I could have told you there are *no* Harshoms in Canada. I happen to know that because –'

'Oh, I'd given up expecting that. Her name wasn't Harshom – it was Gale,' Colin interrupted, with the air of one explaining.

'Indeed. And I suppose it wasn't Ottilie, either?' Dr Harshom said heavily.

'No. It was Belinda,' Colin told him.

The doctor blinked slightly, opened his mouth, and then thought better of it. Colin went on:

'So then I flew over, to make sure. It was the most agonizing journey I've ever made. But it was all right. Just one distant sight of her was enough. I couldn't have *mistaken* her for Ottilie, but she was so very, very nearly Ottilie that I would have known her among ten thousand. Perhaps if her hair and her dress had been –' He paused speculatively, unaware of the expression on the doctor's face. 'Anyway,' he went on. 'I *knew*. And it was damned difficult to stop myself rushing up to her there and then, but I did just have enough sense to hold back.

'Then it was a matter of managing an introduction. After that it was as if there were – well, an inevitability, a sort of predestination about it.'

Curiosity impelled the doctor to say:

'Comprehensible, but sketchy. What, for instance, about her husband?'

'Husband?' Colin looked momentarily startled.

'Well, you did say her name was Gale,' the doctor pointed out.

'So it was, Miss Belinda Gale – I thought I said that. She was engaged once, but she didn't marry. I tell you there was a kind of – well, fate, in the Greek sense, about it.'

'But if –' Dr Harshom began, and then checked himself again. He endeavoured, too, to suppress any sign of scepticism.

'But it would have been just the same if she had had a husband,' Colin asserted, with ruthless conviction. 'He'd have been the wrong man.'

The doctor offered no comment, and he went on:

'There were no complications, or involvements – well, nothing serious. She was living in a flat with her mother, and getting quite a good salary. Her mother looked after the place, and had a widow's pension – her husband was in the R.C.A.F.; shot down over Berlin – so between them they managed to be reasonably comfortable.

'Well, you can imagine how it was. Considered as a phenomenon I wasn't any too welcome to her mother, but she's a fair-minded woman, and we found that, as persons, we liked one another quite well. So that part of it, too, went off more easily than it might have done.'

He paused there. Dr Harshom put in:

'I'm glad to hear it, of course. But I must confess I don't quite see what it has to do with your not bringing your wife along with you.'

Colin frowned.

'Well, I thought – I mean she thought – well, I haven't quite got to the point yet. It's rather delicate.'

'Take your time. After all, I've retired,' said the doctor, amiably.

Colin hesitated.

'All right. I think it'll be fairer to Mrs Gale if I tell it the way it fell out.

'You see, I didn't intend to say anything about what's at the back of all this – about Ottilie, I mean, and why I came to be over in Ottawa – not until later, anyway. You were the only one I had told, and it seemed better that way. . . . I didn't want them wondering if I was a bit off my rocker, naturally. But I went and slipped up.

'It was on the day before our wedding. Belinda was out getting some last-minute things, and I was at the flat doing my best to be reassuring to my future mother-in-law. As nearly as I can recall it, what I said was:

'"My job with E.P.I. is quite a good one, and the prospects are good, but they do have a Canadian end, too, and I dare say that if Ottilie finds she really doesn't like living in England –"

'And then I stopped because Mrs Gale had suddenly sat upright with a jerk, and was staring at me open-mouthed. Then in a shaky sort of voice she asked:

'"*What* did you say?"

'I'd noticed the slip myself, just too late to catch it. So I corrected: "I was just saying that if Belinda finds she doesn't like –"

'She cut in on that.

'"You didn't say Belinda. You said Ottilie."

'"Er – perhaps I did," I admitted, "but, as I say, if she doesn't –"

'"Why?" she demanded. "*Why* did you call her Ottilie?"

'She was intense about that. There was no way out of it.

'"It's, well, it's the way I think of her," I said.

'"But why? *Why* should you think of Belinda as Ottilie?" she insisted.

'I looked at her more carefully. She had gone quite pale, and the hand that was visible was trembling. She was afraid, as well as distressed. I was sorry about that, and I gave up bluffing.

'"I didn't mean this to happen," I told her.

'She looked at me steadily, a little calmer.

'"But now it has, you *must* tell me. What do you know about us?" she asked.

'"Simply that if things had been – different she wouldn't be Belinda Gale. She would be Ottilie Harshom," I told her.

'She kept on watching my face, long and steadily, her own face still pale.

'"I don't understand," she said, more than half to herself. "You *couldn't* know. Harshom – yes, you might have found that out somehow, or guessed it – or did she tell you?" I shook my head. "Never mind, you could find out," she went on. "But Ottilie. . . . You *couldn't* know that – just that one name out of all the thousands of names in the world. . . . *Nobody* knew that – nobody but me. . . ." She shook her head.

'"I didn't even tell Reggie. . . . When he asked me if we could call her Belinda, I said yes; he'd been so very good to me. . . . He had no idea that I had meant to call her Ottilie – nobody had. I've never told anyone, before or since. . . . So how *can* you know?"

'I took her hand between mine, and pressed it, trying to comfort her and calm her.

'"There's nothing to be alarmed about," I told her. "It was a – a dream, a kind of vision – I just knew. . . ."

'She shook her head. After a minute she said quietly:

'"Nobody knew but me. . . . It was in the summer, in 1927. We were on the river, in a punt, pulled under a willow. A white launch swished by us, we watched it go, and saw the name on its stern. Malcolm said"' – if Colin noticed Dr Harshom's sudden start, his only acknowledgement of it was a repetition of the last two words – '"Malcolm said: 'Ottilie – pretty name, isn't it? It's in our family. My father had a sister Ottilie who died when she was a little girl. If ever I have a daughter I'd like to call her Ottilie.'"'

Colin Trafford broke off, and regarded the doctor for a moment. Then he went on:

'After that she said nothing for a long time, until she added:

'"He never knew, you know. Poor Malcolm, he was killed before even I knew she was coming. . . . I did so want to call her Ottilie for him. . . . He'd have liked that. . . . I wish I had. . . ." And then she began quietly crying. . . .'

Dr Harshom had one elbow on his desk, one hand over his eyes. He did not move for some little time. At last he pulled out a handkerchief, and blew his nose decisively.

'I did hear there was a girl,' he said. 'I even made inquiries, but they told me she had married soon afterwards. I thought she – But why didn't she come to me? I would have looked after her.'

'She couldn't know that. She was fond of Reggie Gale. He was in love with her, and willing to give the baby his name,' Colin said.

After a glance towards the desk, he got up and walked over to the window. He stood there for several minutes with his back to the room until he heard a movement behind him. Dr Harshom had got up and was crossing to the cupboard.

'I could do with a drink,' he said. 'The toast will be the restoration of order, and the rout of the random element.'

'I'll support that,' Colin told him, 'but I'd like to couple it with the confirmation of your contention, Doctor – after all, you are right at last, you know; Ottilie Harshom *does not exist* – not any more. – And then, I think, it will be high time you were introduced to your granddaughter, Mrs Colin Trafford.'

A Long Spoon

'I say,' Stephen announced, with an air of satisfaction, 'do you know that if I lace up the tape this way round I can hear myself talking backwards!'

Dilys laid down her book, and regarded her husband. Before him, on the table, stood the tape-recorder, an amplifier, and small sundries. A wandering network of leads connected them to one another, to the mains, to a big loudspeaker in the corner, and to the pair of phones on his head. Lengths and snippets of tape littered half the floor.

'Another triumph of science,' she said, coolly. 'As I understood it, you were just going to do a bit of editing so that we could send a record of the party to Myra. I'm quite sure she'd prefer it the right way round.'

'Yes, but this idea just came to me –'

'And what a mess! It looks as if we'd been giving someone a ticker-tape reception. What is it all?'

Stephen glanced down at the strips and coils of tape.

'Oh, those are just the parts where everybody was talking at once, and bits of that very unfunny story Charles would keep trying to tell everyone – and a few indiscretions, and so on.'

Dilys eyed the litter, as she stood up.

'It must have been a much more indiscreet party than it seemed at the time,' she said. 'Well, you clear it up while I go and put on the kettle.'

'But you must hear this,' he protested.

She paused at the door.

'Give me,' she suggested, 'give me one good reason – just one – why I ought to hear you talk backwards. . . .' And she departed.

Left alone, Stephen made no attempt to gather the debris; instead, he pressed the playback key and listened with interest to the curious gabbeldigook that was his backwards voice. Then he stopped the machine, took off the headphones, and switched over to the loudspeaker. He was interested to find that though the voice still had a European quality it seemed to rattle through its incomprehensible sounds at great speed. Experimentally, he halved the speed, and turned up the volume. The voice, now an octave lower, drawled out deep, ponderous, impossible-sounding syllables in a very impressive way indeed. He nodded to himself and leant his head back, listening to it rolling sonorously around the room.

Suddenly there was a rushing sound, not unlike a reduced facsimile of a locomotive blowing off steam, also a gust of warm air reminiscent of a stokehole. . . .

It took Stephen by surprise so that he jumped, and almost overturned his chair. Recovering, he reached forward, hastily pressing keys and turning knobs. The voice from the loudspeaker cut off abruptly. He peered anxiously into the items of his apparatus, looking for sparks, or smoke. There was neither, but it was while he was in the act of sighing his relief over this that he became, in some way, aware that he was no longer alone in the room. He jerked his head round. His jaw dropped fully an inch, and he sat staring at the figure standing some four feet to his rear right.

The man stood perfectly straight, with his arms pressed closely to his sides. He was tall, quite six feet, and made to look taller still by his hat – a narrow-brimmed, entirely cylindrical object of quite remarkable height. For the rest, he wore a high starched collar with spread points, a grey silk cravat, a long, dark frock-coat with silk facings, and lavender-grey trousers, with the points of black, shiny boots jutting out beneath them. Stephen had to tilt back his head to get a foreshortened view of the face. It was good-looking, bronzed, as if by Mediterranean sun. The eyes were large and dark. A luxuriant moustache swept out to join with well-tended whiskers at the points of the jaw. The chin, and lower parts of the cheeks were closely shaved. The features themselves stirred vague memories of Assyrian sculptures.

Even in the first astonished moment it was borne in upon Stephen that, inappropriate as the ensemble might be to the circumstances, there could be no doubt of its quality, nor, in the proper time and place, of its elegance. He continued to stare.

The man's mouth moved.

'I have come,' he announced, with a pontifical air.

'Er – yes,' said Stephen. 'I – er – I see that, but, well, I don't quite. . . .'

'You called upon me. I have come,' the man repeated, with an air of explaining everything.

Stephen added a frown to his bewilderment.

'But I didn't say a thing,' he protested. 'I was just sitting here, and –'

'There is no need for alarm. I am sure you will not regret it,' said the man.

'I am not alarmed. I'm baffled,' said Stephen. 'I don't see –'

The pontifical quality was reduced by a touch of impatience as the man inquired:

'Did you not construct the Iron Pentacle?' – Without moving his arms, he contracted three fingers of his right hand so that the lavender-gloved forefinger remained pointing downwards. 'Did you not also utter the Word of Power?' he added.

Stephen looked where the finger pointed. He perceived that some of the discarded scraps of tape did make a crude geometrical figure on the floor, just permissibly, perhaps, a kind of pentacle form. But *iron* pentacle, the man had said. . . . Oh, the iron-oxide coating, of course. . . . H'm, pretty near the border of permissibility, too, one would think. . . .

'Word of Power,' though. . . . Well, it was conceivable that a voice talking backwards might stumble upon a Word of practically anything. . . .

'It rather looks,' he said, 'as if there had been a slight mistake – a coincidence. . . .'

'A strange coincidence,' remarked the man, sceptically.

'But isn't that really the thing about coincidences? That they are, I mean,' Stephen pointed out.

'I have never heard of it happening before – never,' said the man. 'Whenever I, or any of my friends, have been summoned in this way, it has been to do business: and business has invariably been done.'

'Business . . . ?' Stephen inquired.

'Business,' the man repeated. 'You have certain needs we can supply. You have a certain object we should like to add to our collection. All that is necessary is that we could come to terms. Then you sign the pact, with your blood, of course, and there it is.'

It was the word 'pact' that touched the spot. Stephen recalled the slight smell of hot clinkers that had pervaded the room.

'Ah, I begin to see,' he said. 'This is a visitation – a raising. You mean that you are Old –'

The man cut in, with a quick frown:

'My name is Batruel. I am one of the fully accredited representatives of my Master; his plenipotentiary, holding his authority to arrange pacts. Now, if you would be so good as to release me from this pentacle which I find an extremely tight fit, we could discuss the terms of the pact much more comfortably.'

Stephen regarded the man for some moments, and then shook his head.

'Ha-ha!' he said. 'Ha-ha! Ha-ha!'

The man's eyes widened. He looked huffed.

'I beg your pardon!'

'Look,' Stephen said. 'I apologize for the accident that brought you here. But let us have it clearly understood that you have come to the wrong place to do any business – the wrong place entirely.'

Batruel studied him thoughtfully. He lifted his head, and his nostrils twitched slightly.

'Very curious,' he remarked. 'I detect no odour of sanctity.'

'Oh, it isn't that,' Stephen assured him. 'It simply is that quite a number of your deals have been pretty well documented by now – and one of the really consistent things about them is that the party of the second part has never failed to regret the deal, in due course.'

'Oh, come! Think what I can offer you –'

Stephen cut him short by shaking his head again.

'Save yourself the trouble,' he advised. 'I have to deal with up-to-date high-pressure salesmen every day.'

Batruel regarded him with a saddened eye.

'I am more used to dealing with the high-pressure customer,' he admitted. 'Well, if you are quite sure that there has been no more than a genuine mistake, I suppose there is nothing to be done but for me to go back and explain. This has not, to my knowledge, ever happened before – though, of course, by the laws of chance it had to happen some time. Just my bad luck. Very well, then. Good-bye – oh, dear, what have I said? – I mean *vale*, my friend. I am ready!'

His stance was already rigid; now, as he closed his eyes, his face became wooden, too.

Nothing happened.

Baturel's jaw relaxed.

'Well, say it!' he exclaimed, testily.

'Say what?' Stephen inquired.

'The other Word of Power, of course. The Dismissal.'

'But I don't know it. I don't know anything about Words of Power,' Stephen protested.

Batruel's brows came lower, and approached one another.

'Are you telling me you cannot send me back?' he inquired.

'If it needs a Word of Power I certainly can't,' Stephen told him.

An expression of dismay came over Batruel's face.

'But this is unheard of. . . . What am I to do? I *must* have either a completed pact, *or* the Word of Dismissal.'

'All right, you tell me the Word, and I'll say it,' Stephen offered.

'But I don't know it,' said Batruel. 'I have never heard it.

Everyone who has summoned me until now has been anxious to do business and sign the pact. . . .' He paused. 'It really would simplify matters very greatly if you could see your way to – No? Oh, dear, this is most awkward. I really don't see what we are going to do. . . .'

There was a sound at the door followed by a couple of taps on it from Dilys's toe, to indicate that she was carrying a tray. Stephen crossed to the door and opened it a preliminary chink.

'We have a visitor,' he warned her. He did not want to see the tray dropped out of sheer surprise.

'But how –?' she began, and then, as he held the door open more widely, she almost did drop the tray. Stephen took it from her while she stood staring, and set it down safely.

'Darling, this is Mr Batruel – my wife,' he said.

Batruel, still standing rigidly straight, now looked embarrassed as well as constrained. He turned his head in her direction, and nodded it slightly.

'Charmed, Ma'am,' he said. 'I would have you excuse my style, but my movements are unhappily constricted. If your husband would do me the courtesy of breaking this pentacle. . . .'

Dilys went on staring at him, and running an appraising eye over his clothes.

'I – I'm afraid I don't understand,' she complained.

Stephen did his best to explain the situation. At the end, she said:

'Well, I really don't know. . . . We shall have to see what can be done, shan't we? It's so difficult – not as if he were just an ordinary D.P., I mean.' She went on regarding Batruel thoughtfully, and then added: 'Steve, if you have made it really clear to him that we're not signing anything, don't you think you might let him out of it? He does look so uncomfortable there.'

'I thank you, Ma'am. I am indeed uncomfortable,' Batruel said, gratefully.

Stephen considered.

'Well, since he is here anyway, and we know where we stand, perhaps it won't do any harm,' he conceded. He bent down, and brushed aside some of the tape on the floor.

Batruel stepped out of the disrupted pentacle. With his right hand he removed his hat; with his left, he gave a touch to his cravat. He turned to sweep Dilys a bow, doing it beautifully, too; toe pointed, left hand on a non-existent hilt, hat held over his heart.

'Your servant, Ma'am.'

He repeated the exercise in Stephen's direction.

'Your servant, Sir.'

Stephen's response was well-intentioned, but he was aware that it showed inadequately against his visitor's style. There followed an awkward pause. Dilys broke it by saying:

'I'd better fetch another cup.'

She went out, returned, and presided.

'You – er – you've not visited England lately, Mr Batruel?' she suggested, socially.

Batruel looked mildly astonished.

'What makes you think that, Mrs Tramon?' he asked.

'Oh, I – I just thought . . .' Dilys said, vaguely.

'My wife is thinking of your clothes,' Stephen told him. 'Furthermore, if you will excuse my mentioning it, you get your periods somewhat mixed. The style of your bow, for instance, precedes that of your clothes by, well, at least two generations, I should say.'

Batruel looked a little taken aback. He glanced down at himself. 'I paid particular note to the fashion last time I was here,' he said, with disappointment. Dilys broke in.

'Don't let him upset you, Mr Batruel. They are beautiful clothes – and such quality of material.'

'But not quite in the current *ton*?' said Batruel, acutely.

'Well, not quite,' Dilys admitted. 'I expect you get a bit out of touch in – where you live.'

'Perhaps we do,' Batruel confessed. 'We used to do quite a deal of business in these parts up to the seventeenth and eighteenth centuries, but during the nineteenth it fell off badly. There's always a little, of course, but it is a matter of chance who is on call for different districts, and it so happens that I myself visited here only once during the nineteenth century, and not at all during the present century, until now. So you can imagine what a pleasure it was to me to receive your husband's summons; with what high hopes of a mutually beneficial transaction I presented myself –'

'Now, now! That's enough of that . . .' Stephen broke in.

'Oh, yes, of course. My apologies. The old war-horse scenting battle, you understand.'

There was a pause. Dilys regarded the visitor pensively. To one who knew her as well as her husband did, it was clear that there was a half-hearted struggle going on, and that curiosity was being allowed to pile up the points. At last she said:

'I hope your English assignments have not always been a disappointment to you, Mr Batruel?'

'Oh, by no means, Ma'am. I have the happiest recollections of visits to your country. I remember calling upon an Adept who lived near Winchester – it would be somewhere in the middle of the sixteenth century, I think – he wanted a prosperous estate, a title, and a beautiful, well-born wife. We were able to fix him up with a very nice place not far from Dorchester – his descendants hold it to this day, I believe. Then there was another, quite a young man, early in the eighteenth century, who was set upon a nice income, and the opportunity to marry into court circles. We gave satisfaction there, and his blood now runs in some very surprising places. And just a few years later there was another young man, a rather dull fellow who simply wanted to become a famous playwright and wit. That's more difficult, but we managed it. I shouldn't be surprised to find his name remembered still. He was –'

'That's all very well,' Stephen broke in. 'Nice enough for the descendants, but what happened to the protagonists?'

Batruel lifted his shoulders slightly.

'Well, a bargain is a bargain. A contract freely entered into . . .' he said, reprovingly. 'Although I have not been here myself lately,' he went on, 'I understand from my fellow representatives that requirements, though they differ in details, are much the same in principle. Titles are still popular, particularly with the wives of clients. So, too, the entrée to society – such as it has become. So is a fine country house, and nowadays, of course, we supply it with all mod. con., also a *pied-à-terre* in Mayfair. Where we used to provide a full stable we now offer a Bent-Rollsley saloon, a private aircraft perhaps . . .' he continued with a dreamy air.

Stephen felt it time to break in.

'Bent-Rollsley, indeed! You'd better read your Consumer Research handbook more carefully next time. And now I'll be obliged if you will leave off tempting my wife. She's not the one who would have to pay for it.'

'No,' Batruel agreed. 'That's a feature of woman's life. She always has to pay something, but the more she gets the less it costs her. Now your wife would have a much easier life, no work to do, servants to –'

'Will you please stop it!' Stephen told him. 'It should be clear to you by now that your system is old-fashioned. We've got wise to it. It's lost its appeal.'

Batruel looked doubtful.

'According to our bulletins the world is still a very wicked place,' he objected.

'I dare say, but the wickeder part of it hasn't any use for your old-fashioned terms. It greatly prefers to get a lot for a little if it can't get something for nothing.'

'Scarcely ethical,' murmured Batruel. 'One should have standards.'

'That may be, but there it is. Besides, we are much more closely knit now. How do you think I'd be able to square a sudden title with Debrett, or sudden affluence with the Income Tax inspectors, or even a sudden mansion with the Planning Authority. One must face facts.'

'Oh, I expect all that could be managed all right,' Batruel said.

'Well, it isn't going to be. There is only one way nowadays that a man can safely become suddenly rich. It's – by Jove. . . !' He broke off abruptly, and plunged into thought.

Batruel said to Dilys:

'It is such a pity your husband is not doing himself justice. He has great potentialities. One can see that at a glance. Now, with some capital behind him there would be such opportunities, such scope. . . . And the world still has so much to offer to a rich man – and to his wife, of course – respect, authority, ocean-going yachts. . . . One can't help feeling he is being wasted at present. . . .'

Dilys glanced at her abstracted husband.

'You feel that about him, too? I've often thought that they don't appreciate him properly in the business. . . .'

'Office politics, very likely,' said Batruel. 'Many a young man's gifts are stunted by them. But with independence and a helpful wife – if I may say so, a clever and beautiful young wife – to help him, I see no reason why he should not –'

Stephen's attention had returned.

'Straight out of the Tempter's Manual; Chapter One, I should think,' he remarked scornfully. 'Now just lay off it, will you, and try to look facts in the face. Once you have grasped them, I am prepared to consider doing business with you.'

Batruel's expression brightened a little.

'Ah,' he said, 'I thought that when you had had a little time to consider the advantages of our offer –'

Stephen interrupted.

'Look,' he said. 'The first fact you have to face is that I have no use whatever for your usual terms – so you might as well stop trying to form a pressure-group with my wife.

'The second fact is this: *you're* the one who is in a jam, not me. How do you propose ever to get back to – er – well, wherever you come from, if I don't help you?'

'All I'm suggesting is that you help yourself at the same time that you help me,' Batruel pointed out.

'Got only one angle about this, haven't you? Now, listen to me. I can see three possible courses before us. One: we find someone who can give us this Word of Power for your dismissal. Do you know how we set about that? – No? Well, nor do I.

'Then, two: I could ask the Vicar round here to have a shot at exorcizing you. I expect he'd be quite glad to oblige. It might even lead to his being canonized later on for resisting temptation. . . .'

Batruel shuddered.

'Certainly not,' he objected. 'A friend of mine was once exorcized back in the fifteenth century. He found it excruciatingly painful at the time, and he hasn't fully regained confidence in himself yet.'

'Very well, then, there's still a third possibility. In consideration of a nice round sum of money, with no strings attached, I will undertake to find someone willing to make a pact with you. Then when you have it safely signed, you will be able to report back with your mission honourably completed. How does that strike you?'

'No good at all,' Batruel replied promptly. 'You are simply trying to get two concessions out of us for the price of one. Our accountants would never sanction it.'

Stephen shook his head sadly.

'It's no wonder to me that your practice is slipping. In all the thousands of years you've been in business, you don't seem to have got a step beyond the idea of a first mortgage. And you're even prepared to employ your own capital when you should be using somebody else's. That's no way to get ahead. Now, under my scheme, I get some money, you get your pact, and the only capital laid out is a few shillings from me.'

'I don't see how that can be,' Batruel said, doubtfully.

'I assure you it can. It may mean your having to stay for a few weeks, but we can put you up in the spare room. Now, do you play football?'

'Football?' Batruel repeated vaguely. 'I don't think so. How does it go?'

'Well you'll have to mug up on the principles and tactics of the game. But the important point is this: a player must kick with precision. Now, if the ball is not exactly where he calculated it will be, this precision is lost, so is the opportunity, and so, eventually, the game. Have you got that?'

'I think so.'

'Then you will appreciate that just a nudge of an inch or so to the ball at a critical moment could do a lot – there wouldn't need to be any unsporting roughstuff, or mayhem. The outcome of a game could be arranged quite unsuspiciously. All it would need would be a nicely timed nudge by one of those imps you use for the practical jobs. That shouldn't be very difficult for you to arrange.'

'No,' Batruel agreed. 'It should be quite simple. But I don't quite see –'

'Your trouble, old man, is that you are hopelessly out of touch with modern life, in spite of your bulletins,' Stephen told him. 'Dilys, where is that Pools entry-form?'

Half an hour later Batruel was showing an appreciative grasp of the possibilities.

'Yes, I see,' he said. 'With a little study of the technicalities it should not be difficult to produce a loss, or a draw, perhaps even a win, as required.'

'Exactly,' approved Stephen. 'Well, there you are. I fill in the coupon – laying out several shillings on it to make it look better. You fix the matches. And I collect handsomely – without any awkward tax questions.'

'That's all very well for you,' Batruel pointed out, 'but I don't see how it is going to get me my pact, unless you –'

'Ah, now. Here we come to the next stage,' Stephen told him. 'In return, I undertake to find you a pact-signer in, shall we say, six weeks? in exchange for my winnings. Will that do? Good. Then let's have an agreement about it. Dilys, bring me a sheet of writing-paper, will you, and some blood – oh, no, stupid of me, we've got blood. . . .'

Five weeks later Stephen slid his Bentley to a stop in front of the Northpark Hotel, and a moment later Batruel came down the steps. The idea of putting him up at home had had to be abandoned after a couple of days. His impulse to tempt was in the nature of an uncontrollable reflex, and proved to be incompatible with domestic tranquillity, so he had removed to a hotel where he found the results less inconvenient, and the opportunities more varied.

He emerged from the revolving door cutting a very different figure from that of his first appearance in Stephen's sitting-room. The side-whiskers had gone, though the luxuriant moustache remained. The frock-coat had been replaced by a meticulously cut grey suit, the remarkable top-hat by a grey felt, the cravat by a tie with stripes that were discreetly not quite Guards. Indeed, he now presented the appearance of a comfortably-placed, good-looking, latter twentieth-century man of about forty.

'Hop in,' Stephen told him. 'You've got the pact-form with you?'

Batruel patted his pocket.

'I always carry it. You never know . . .' he said, as they set off.

The first time Stephen had picked up the treble-chance win there had been, in spite of his hope of remaining anonymous, considerable publicity. It is less easy than it might seem to hide a windfall of £220,000. He and Dilys had taken the precaution of going into hiding before the next win was due – this time for £210,000. There had been some hesitation when it came to paying him the third cheque – £225,000 – not exactly a quibbling, for there was nothing to quibble about; the forecasts were down in ink, but there was a thoughtfulness on the part of the promoters which caused them to send representatives to see him. One of these, an earnest young man in glasses, talked with some intensity about the laws of chance, and had then produced a figure with a staggering number of noughts which he claimed to represent the odds against anyone bringing off a treble-chance three times.

Stephen was interested. His system, he said, must be even better than he had thought to win against such an astronomical unlikelihood as that.

The young man wanted to know about his system. Stephen, however, had declined to talk about it – but he had indicated that he might not be unwilling to discuss some aspects of it with the head of Gripshaw's Pools. So here they were now, on their way to an interview with Sam Gripshaw himself.

The Pools head office stood beside one of the new outer roads, set a little back behind a smooth lawn decorated with beds of salvias. Stephen was saluted by a braided porter as he slid his car into its park. A few moments later they were being shown into a spacious private office where Sam Gripshaw was on his feet to greet them. Stephen shook hands and introduced his companion.

'This is Mr Batruel, my adviser,' he explained.

Sam Gripshaw's glance at Batruel suddenly turned into a careful, searching look. He appeared to become thoughtful for a moment. Then he turned back to Stephen.

'Well, first, I should congratulate you, young man. You're by a long way the biggest winner in the whole history of the Pools. Six hundred and fifty-five thousand pounds, they tell me – very tidy, very tidy indeed. But' – he shook his head – 'it can't go on, you know. It can't go on. . . .'

'Oh, I wouldn't say that,' Stephen replied amiably, as they sat down.

Again Sam Gripshaw shook his head.

'Once is good luck; twice could be extraordinarily good luck; three times gives off a pretty funny smell; four times would rock the industry; five times would just about bust it. Nobody's going to put up even his few bob against dead certs. Stands to reason. Now you've got a system you say?'

'*We've* got a system,' Stephen corrected. 'My friend, Mr Batruel –'

'Ah, yes – Mr Batruel,' said Sam Gripshaw, looking at Batruel thoughtfully again. 'I suppose you wouldn't like to tell me a little about your system?'

'You can scarcely expect us to do *that*. . .' Stephen protested.

'No, I suppose not,' Sam Gripshaw admitted. 'All the same, you might as well. You can't go on with it –'

'Because if we were to, we'd bust your industry? Well, we don't want to do that, of course. In fact that is why we are here. Mr Batruel has a proposition to put to you.'

'Let's hear it,' said Mr Gripshaw.

Batruel rose to his feet.

'You have a very fine business here, Mr Gripshaw. It would be most unfortunate if it were to lose the confidence of the public – both for them, and for yourself. I don't need to stress that, for I perceive that you have refrained from giving any publicity to my friend, Mr Tramon's, third win. Very wise of you, Sir, if I may say so. It could initiate a subtle breath of despondency. . . .

'Now, I am in the fortunate position of being able to propose a means by which the risk of such a situation occurring again can be positively eliminated. It will not cost you a penny, and yet . . .' He launched himself into his temptation with the air of an artist taking up his beloved brush. Sam Gripshaw heard him through patiently to his conclusion:

'– and, in return for this – this mere formality, I am willing to undertake that neither our friend, Mr Stephen Tramon, here, nor anyone else will receive any further assistance in er – prognostication from me. The emergency will then be over, and you will then be able to pursue your business with the confidence that I am sure it so well merits.'

He produced his form of Pact with a flourish, and laid it on the desk.

Sam Gripshaw reached for it, and glanced through it. Rather to Stephen's surprise, he nodded, almost without hesitation.

'Seems straight enough,' he said. 'I can see I'm not well placed to argue. All right. I'll sign.'

Batruel smiled happily. He stepped forward, with a small, convenient penknife in his hand.

When the signing was done Sam Gripshaw wrapped a clean handkerchief round his forearm. Batruel picked up the pact and took a step back, waving it gently to dry the signature.

Then he inspected it with simple pleasure, folded it with care, and placed it in his pocket.

He beamed upon them both. In his elation, his sense of period slipped again. He made his elegant eighteenth-century bow.

'Your servant, gentlemen.'

And, abruptly, he was gone, leaving nothing but the faintest trace of sulphur on the air.

It was Sam Gripshaw who broke the following silence.

'Well, that's got rid of *him* – and he can't get back until somebody raises him,' he added, with satisfaction. He turned to contemplate Stephen. 'You've not done so badly, young man, have you? *You* pocket more than half a million for selling him *my* soul. That's what I call business ability. Wish I'd had more of it when I was younger.'

'Well, you, at any rate, don't seem to be very perturbed about it,' Stephen said, with a perceptible note of relief in his voice.

'No. Doesn't worry me,' Mr Gripshaw told him. '*He's* the one who's going to be worried. Makes you think, doesn't it? Thousands of years him and his lot have been in business – and *still* got no system into it. What you need today is organization – the whole business at your finger-tips so you know where you are, and what's what. Too old-fashioned by half, that lot. Time they got some efficiency experts on to it.'

'Well, not very subtle perhaps,' agreed Stephen. 'But then, his need *is* rather specialized, and he *has* got what he was after.'

'Huh! You wait till he's had time to look in the files – if they know what files are down there. How do you think I ever managed to raise enough capital to start this place . . . ?'

Other books by John Wyndham, published
in Penguins, are described overleaf

John Wyndham

The Day of the Triffids
The Day of the Triffids is a fantastic, frightening, but entirely plausible story of the future when the world is dominated by triffids, grotesque and dangerous plants over seven feet tall.†

The Kraken Wakes
The title is taken from a poem by Tennyson, and the book tells of the awakening and rise to power of forces from beneath the surface of the sea. The almost imperceptible beginnings and the cruelly terrifying consequences of this threat to the world are seen through the eyes of a radio script-writer and his wife.*

The Chrysalids
A thrilling and realistic account of the world beset by genetic mutations. 'Jolly good story, well-conceived community, characters properly up to simple requirements. Better than the *Kraken*, perhaps even the *Triffids*' – Observer*

The Seeds of Time
The ten stories making up this book are acknowledged by their author as 'experiments in adapting the SF motif to various styles of short story'. The fascinating variety here does much to explain John Wyndham's success.*

The Midwich Cuckoos
This is the book from which the film *The Village of the Damned* was made.*

Trouble With Lichen
The story of a Cambridge scientist's agonizing decision to conceal his discovery of a limited supply of an antidote to old age. 'If even a tenth of science fiction were as good, we should be in clover' – Kingsley Amis in the Observer*

The Outward Urge (with Lucas Parkes)
With technical collaboration, John Wyndham excitingly plots the conquest of Space.*

* Not for sale in the U.S.A.
† Not for sale in the U.S.A. or Canada

For a complete list of books available please write to Penguin Books whose address can be found on the back of the title page